The White Isle

Lavinia of Britain

The White Isle

Caroline Dale Snedeker

HILLSIDE EDUCATION

Cover image from the 1940 first edition
"Lavinia of Britain" by Eve Fitzpatrick
Cover and interior book design by Mary Jo Loboda

ISBN: 978-1-955402-22-4

Hillside Education
475 Bidwell Hill Road
Lake Ariel, PA 18436
www.hillsideeducation.com

CITIES AND RIVERS OF THE JOURNEY

Ancient Name	Modern Name
Aqua Sulis	Bath
Arausio	Orange
Arlate	Arles in France
Arnus River	Arno
Augustodunum	Antun
Avenio	Avignon
Caledonia	Scotland
Caleva	Silchester
Corinium	Cirencester
Dubris or Dubrae	Dover
Durocortorum	Rheims
Eboricum	York
Forum Julii	Frejus
Fretum Gallicum	English Channel
Genua	Genoa
Gessoriacum	Boulogne
Glevum	Gloucester
Isca Dumnores	Exeter
Isca Salures	Carleon upon Usk
Ivernia	Ireland
Londinium	London
Lugdunum	Lyons
Monoecus	Monoco and Monte Carlo
Nimausis	Nimes
Noviodunum	Soissons
Pisae	Pisa
River Rhodanus	Rhone River
River Thamisis	Thames

Author's Note

THE DATE of the destruction of the Ninth Legion is not exactly known. But it is supposed to be before Hadrian's visit to Britain. And that he brought with him the Sixth Legion to take its place. I have taken the liberty of destroying the Ninth Legion after Hadrian's visit.

The mosaic pavements depicting Orpheus were common in Britain. The pavement with the chalices in the corners was not an Orpheus but a god sitting on a tiger and was found in London.

Caroline Dale Snedeker

The White Isle

CHAPTER ONE

N THE CITY of Rome on the edge of the Palatine Hill lived Lavinia, daughter of Publius Favonius Claudius. She was a happy young girl. She considered that she lived in the most fortunate place in the whole world— Rome, the Eternal City, and on the Clivus Victoriae, the most honorable street in Rome. Very few people lived on the Palatine. In the olden days when Rome first began everybody lived there—everybody that is who counted. Then came the Emperor Augustus who built his huge palace of marble on the summit. After that every succeeding emperor had made the palace bigger, added new palaces, halls, temples, gardens, until the whole hill was covered and only the edges of the hill remained for the proud folk of old.

The house where Lavinia lived was ancient. The atrium contained no handsome fountain, only a pool with the square roof hole above it so the rain could run in. Rain water was sweet to taste—no water like it—and Lavinia loved the drip and tinkle of the rain in her pool. The Claudian family, her branch of it, had lived here so long that no one knew who had

1

been the first to live there. On the small altar in the atrium corner stood always the tiny statue of the genius of the house. It was a stiff bearded figure with his toga drawn reverently over his head. He looked like her father except for the beard. Every morning they sacrificed to him, and Lavinia thought that in the dim past he had built the house and blessed it so it would be theirs forever.

Lavinia was plain-featured. But until a certain strange day in early February she had not known that she was homely. She knew that her mother loved her. And though she could not think of her father in connection with love she knew he approved her and thought her a worthy daughter of the house. She knew that she learned her lessons quickly and could even help Marcus who was two years older. And once her mother, who seldom praised, said, "Daughter, I believe you weave the best cloth of any maiden on the hill."

So why should Lavinia not be content?

The February day had begun happily enough. Her mother, Aurelia, was going to sacrifice at the temple of Vesta and asked Lavinia to go with her. Lavinia loved anything that was out of doors. Everything she had to do was in the house. If she learned her lessons, it was in the house. If she spun or wove, it was in the house. If she helped mother with the slaves—always in the house. For, being a girl, the house was her place and Lavinia took that for granted. But when she was to go outdoors her heart always sang within her. Now she knew she would go down the hill to the Forum. Perhaps after the sacrifice Mother would take her to the flower market and buy her flowers. Lavinia had never picked flowers herself, but to hold them brought her more happiness than almost any other thing. She sang softly under her breath as she went to her room. "Come Ino," she called.

2

Then Ino bathed her in warm water, put on her best white tunic and her best toga. She drew the edge of the toga up over Lavinia's head.

"You must hold it tight, darling," she said, "for it's a cold windy day."

Then came Aurelia in her cloak, the two slaves carrying gifts and incense, Aurelia's special slave, Clotho, and Ino, Lavinia's slave, and they went out. The wind met them cold and ungentle as Lavinia loved it; the great arch of the sky which one always sees from the top of a hill made her heart feel big and roomy and free. It was a sunny day with white clouds racing before the wind, and the sky as blue as summer. Far down the valley Lavinia could see the gleaming tiled roofs of the Forum, the columns by the open squares, a splash of color for the flower market, and a tiny procession (there were always processions in the Forum), shimmering with upheld spears and golden symbols of some god.

They started down the hill. They never once looked back at the great piled-up walls of the Imperial palace with its literal thousand windows, its roofs set this way and that, and its confusion of terraces. One might almost think they disliked the palace.

Down they went the zigzag way and in a few minutes were at the temple. Of course, no word was spoken, for all kept silence before sacrifice. After the sacrifice they went across into the College of Vestals to call upon Aunt Aurelia for whom Mother was named. They were all very proud of Aunt Aurelia as who would not be with a Vestal Virgin in the family. But Lavinia was a little afraid of her and was glad to be left in the courtyard watching the fountain blown sidewise, making wet the flags with its spray.

Then Mother and Aunt Aurelia came out and Lavinia

suddenly realized they were anxious.

"Favonius should be careful," said Aunt Aurelia in her proud, low voice.

"Yes," said Mother; then her head lifted. "After all, I am proud of the Claudian spirit. It is not any one thing that Favonius has done. It is himself, a citizen of the Republic— all his spirit and thought go back to that, and of course, his actions. No amount of empire or emperors can change him."

"Careful!" Aunt Aurelia's lips repeated the word but she did not even whisper. She laid her hand protectingly on Mother's shoulder.

The wind had increased. As the great door of the Vestal College closed behind them, a gust caught Lavinia's toga, swept it aloft from her head. Lavinia spun around catching it with both hands, fearing for the moment that she might be left with only her tunic in the street.

As she turned she met full-face two young men. She knew who they were though she had not met them—Quintus, who lived next door, and Decimus, his best friend. She saw Quintus whisper to Decimus, and immediately Decimus began to stare into her face.

"What a chance!" he said loudly. "By Pollux, she's as ugly as a slave from Gaul. I'll have none of her."

Quintus laughed. "You have no choice," he said.

"I shall make choice," declared Decimus.

Mother hurriedly stepped in front of Lavinia. But it was too late. Lavinia had heard. She looked up at her mother, her face puckered with wonder and misery.

"Never mind," spoke Mother. "We all know how rude Quintus' friends are."

"But why did he notice me? Why did he say 'what a chance!'"

"I don't know, daughter. It was all a part of his rudeness."

Lavinia could see that her mother was as puzzled as she herself. They began to hurry toward the hill.

"Mother," Lavinia persisted, "why did he say I was ugly? Am I ugly?"

"No, daughter, no—of course not." Mother was white with anger. "How dared he!" she kept saying to herself. "In the open street, how dared he!" But somehow Lavinia knew that what Decimus said was true.

Silently she walked beside her mother who now held her hand. They stopped for no flowers. Indeed, Lavinia had forgotten all about them, and the way Mother held her hand so tight she knew even Mother was afraid. But Lavinia was not afraid. At least not of Decimus. She was afraid of what he had said. Could it be that it was true? Oh, why had she never thought about it before?

"Ugly—ugly." The word rang in her mind and his horrid voice saying it, "Ugly as a slave from Gaul."

In the house Mother kissed her. "Now, Lavinia," she said almost severely, "I want you to forget Decimus' words. He is a rude, bad young man. Don't you remember hearing him cursing his slave in the garden next door? Nothing that he does is right, and nothing that he says is true."

"Yes, Mother," said Lavinia so quietly that Aurelia was deceived. Indeed, Aurelia had her own cares that day to occupy her. But Lavinia stole into her mother's bedroom and fetched from there the polished metal mirror. In her own room she gazed and gazed into it.

Yes, of course, she was homely. Her nose was far too long and her mouth much too large for a girl, her cheeks how pale and what cheek bones! She had once heard Ino laughingly say, "Little mistress looks like Julius Caesar." Well, Julius Caesar was a god. Lavinia had thought nothing of it; now she knew that Ino had been making fun of her. Lavinia did not take into account that her eyes were wide and honest, nor that her mouth had the friendliest smile of any girl on the hill. It was not smiling now. It was trembling as she tried not to cry, and her eyes were full of tears. No—it was no use; she could not see her face in the mirror any more.

Favonius Claudius came home early in the afternoon, being urgently summoned by Aurelia his wife. Together they sat for an hour in the farthest end of the garden talking earnestly—question and answer—in low voices. Lavinia did not even notice it; she went to bed and covered herself all up, and Ino thought she was coming down with the fever which was beginning early this year in the slave quarters of Rome.

Next morning Aurelia called her daughter into the garden. Her face was sad, and when Lavinia looked up, questioning, her mother suddenly bent and kissed her forehead.

"I have something to tell you, Lavinia. You must not mind. You know all girls have to be married some day."

Lavinia did not speak for a moment; when she did, it was almost with confidence.

"But, oh, I am not going to be married. Am I, Mother? I am too young."

"You are young, my dear. I have told Father that, but he says—he says—"

Mother stopped and bowed her head low. Lavinia saw she could not go on for tears.

"Mother, Mother," she cried, terrified. She crept close. She climbed into her mother's lap, for all that she was thirteen years old. The words of the young man Decimus came ringing back again in her mind. Her arms clung about Aurelia's neck.

"I know, I know," she cried out. "It's Decimus. Oh, please say it isn't Decimus."

But Mother did not speak nor deny it. She only held Lavinia close and they sobbed together. Presently she lifted her head.

"You know, daughter, that Decimus belongs to one of the richest families in Rome. His father, Rullianus, is an upright, honest man—well liked—well liked by everybody and, yes, by the Emperor too. It was the present Emperor who advanced him to the Senatorial class. The family is plebeian but your father and he became friends in the army when Father was in Egypt. It is a chance we cannot let pass—we cannot let pass—because—because—"

Aurelia's voice trailed into silence, and Lavinia thought that this was because she herself was neither pretty nor wealthy and therefore it was not easy to get her a husband.

"But, Mother, I don't want a husband," she insisted. "I want to stay with you always, always."

At this Mother wept afresh. But she soon stopped herself as if by force and made herself speak.

"Lavinia, my dear daughter, if you are the wife of Decimus, you can help Father as no one else can. Rullianus has influence with the Emperor—one of the few honest men who has. He can later get an appointment for Father. If you belong to, well, if our families are connected, he will not forget; he will want to work for Father and bring us back—and—and don't you want to help Father?"

But Lavinia did not answer. She could not bring herself to say that she wanted to marry Decimus for any reason. That angry voice cursing the poor slave next door. That was Decimus' voice. How could Father want her to marry such a man?

"Decimus' mother is kind. She will be good to you," Mother's voice went on, trying to be steady.

"I don't want Decimus' mother; I want my own dear

darling mother; I want—"

"Be still, dear, while I tell you." Aurelia seemed to push herself to still greater effort to speak.

"I am going to tell you all. If you are old enough to be given in marriage you are old enough to understand. Father has need of help now. The Emperor—the new Emperor, Hadrian—wants to enlarge his palace."

Lavinia looked up, forgetting her tears, wondering at this strange turn in Mother's talk and the earnestness of her mother's voice.

"The only place left is our street, Clivus Victoriae, so he is going to take that. He will build great arches over the street and carry his terraces on top of them."

"But we will have no light," broke in Lavinia.

"We will need no light," said Aurelia bitterly. "For Hadrian will tear down our house and destroy all the houses on the street. When he sent this word, your father cursed the messenger with awful curses and said he would never give up his house. The messenger returned to the Emperor frightened out of his wits. It is the wonder of the gods that the Emperor did not kill your father then. But he still has some little awe of the oldest patrician families in Rome. Instead—instead—" Mother closed her eyes as if praying, then opened them again. "Instead he has appointed your father *legatus euridicus* in Britain." Lavinia's eyes widened with fear. "And, yes, we have to go there—yes, Father and I and Marcus. We will lose all touch with Rome. But if you are here and part of the Rullianus family—dear daughter, you have always been so wise and lovable. The Rullianus family will love you and protect you. You will win them, I know. You will soon grow older. Marcus cannot stay; no one can stay but you. Oh, my poor child!"

Mother almost broke down again and she held Lavinia

close, knowing that now, slowly, surely, she would realize the truth. They were all going away; she, Lavinia, must stay on in Rome in a strange family. Lavinia could only sit in Mother's lap and tremble and shake. She said not a word more. Somehow in those slow moments she seemed to grow older. To be not thirteen years old but thirteen times thirteen. Upon her young shoulders settled the great responsibility. She must make it possible for all to come back to Rome. She must rise up to this.

"The betrothal will be very soon." Mother could hardly say that. "As soon as the unlucky days are over—on The Caristia. Then the next day the wedding. It will be a beautiful wedding, the *conferreato manus*." (This was the highest, most honorable ceremony known in Rome and the most binding.) "Yes, beautiful. You will wear the flame-colored veil and ride through the Forum scattering nuts from the chariot to the poor little boys of the street. You will—"

But Mother's voice again trailed away, ashamed, into silence. She knew Lavinia did not care for the flame-colored veil—nor the pomp and show in the Forum. She knew that Lavinia was only thinking how dearly she loved Father and Brother. She took Lavinia's face in her two hands and gazed at her.

And it seemed to the mother that her daughter was no longer homely. She had the beauty of one who sees a stern deed to be done and has the strength to do it.

CHAPTER TWO

T IS SO STRANGE about the days! Sometimes they seem to go fast and again so slowly, the very same days. Thus it was with the days that followed now. They seemed to step, sorrowful and heavy, into the abyss of time. Again they seemed to race like horses in the stadium to the goal which was Lavinia's wedding day.

There was so much to do. The world of things to be made ready for the journey. Their whole Roman life to be rolled up like a book that is finished. Mother's sisters came and she gave them the heavy carved furniture which had been part of her dowry. Mother's necklace of enamel she gave to Lavinia, for what use would that be in the frontier country of Britain? Father gave her the marble carved table with lion heads on the legs, one of the few things saved when their fortune was lost so long ago. Lavinia was to have five slaves as part of her meager dowry. Twenty-five others would go to Britain and the rest were to be sold. For money was needed for the journey. All day long could be heard their wails through the house. For most of these men and women had been born to the Claudian family.

And the dear house itself. Lavinia went from room to room, unbelieving that anything which had been the same since the beginning of all things could be destroyed, so that it would never be again. She was glad the Rullianus house was far away in the city, so she might never pass here and see the change.

These days of February were the last days of the year. The Romans considered them very unlucky. On the Palatine was an ancient well. Lavinia knew it from old, where the ghosts of the dead were supposed to hide. A stone covered the top to keep them down. Three days in the year the stone was taken off and the ghosts could come out. Old Ino said she had seen them on those nights, and now from February thirteenth to twenty-first was a solemn festival for the dead. Of course no one would start anything, marriage or journey, at such an unlucky time. But on the very day after, as Aurelia had said, Lavinia would be betrothed; that was promised by the two fathers, Decimus' father and hers. Then the next day, February twenty-third, she would be married. After that as soon as possible the Claudian family would go away. For the unlucky days would begin again early in March, and besides, it was well for Claudius to depart quickly while the Emperor was still lenient.

Then like a flash the betrothal day was upon them, the marriage tomorrow. For once in her life Lavinia was the center of everything. She was taken to a certain garden where she gathered with her own hands the flowers which were necessary for a bride to hold. Presents came to her from Father's and Mother's friends—powder-and-paint boxes, and a metal mirror like Mother's. "How foolish," thought Lavinia, "for me to have a mirror."

Decimus gave her a gold ring. He brought it himself and talked affably to Father. He was not a bad-looking young man, and Father was much pleased with him.

As night came on, the eve of the wedding, Lavinia made sacrifice at the little altar in the corner of the atrium. She gave to the *lares* and *penates* her dolls and a tiny wagon she had saved from childhood. She took from her neck a golden locket, her bulla, which had been put there for her protection when she was eight days old, and gave it especially to the tiny man with the beard.

Now she went to bed. Ino and Mother put upon her a long rich toga—the toga *praetexta*—which was indeed her wedding dress. She must sleep in it for good luck. Ino sat by her all night to be sure that she did not wrinkle or crease it in her sleep. But Lavinia had no sleep; she lay there hour after hour very quiet. Sometimes Ino crooned to her the old Greek songs she knew. Sometimes Mother came in and kissed her. Long before day Lavinia knew the priests were making sacrifice in the temple near by and examining the bleeding victims to see if she and Decimus would have good luck this day. For a while she had hoped they would find some ill omen and stop the wedding. But she knew that was wicked—for must she not marry and stay in Rome for Father's sake?

Long before dawn Mother came to finish dressing her for the wedding. They lighted torches and lamps, many of them, so as to have plenty of light—and a fire in a brazier to warm the room. Mother parted her hair in six braids—for all brides must have it so.

"Dear daughter," said Aurelia, "I am glad that your hair is so thick. When I was married mine would hardly last out for six braids." She tied each braid with a bright ribbon. Then came the flame-colored veil—the *flammeum,* oh, a beautiful thing, thin and delicate, though of wool—its rich color shining even by torchlight. Mother had worn it long ago. It went over Lavinia's head and down to her feet but did not cover her face.

Now it was time to go out into the atrium and sit in the grand carved chair at the banquet table. The feast was spread, the slaves hurrying with the last things. The solemn priests came with the two pelts of the lambs just sacrificed. "The omens were lucky," they said and spread the pelts on two seats which were at the left of the little altar which Lavinia knew so well. Here she and Decimus were to sit before they stood up and clasped hands and she must say, "*Quando tu Gaius, ego Gaia,*" which meant that wherever was Decimus there she would be—and belong entirely to him.

Oh, she knew everything she had to do. She was no longer afraid but sat in a strange spaceful quiet. She seemed already married, the long, long day already over and the evening arrived when she must go forth with the marriage procession into the street and hear the shout Terricina, Terricina. The call was so ancient that nobody knew what it meant, but the people in the street always shouted it; Lavinia had heard it several times.

All this while she was in a wide, safe dream where nothing could reach her. She wished she could hold Mother's hand. But she must sit quite alone upon her chair until Decimus came and sat beside her.

Now the day dawned so the guests began to arrive—ever so many—the proudest people in Rome. She could see that Father was pleased that his friends gathered about him in spite of the Emperor's disfavor.

Father had done nothing disgraceful. How often had

Mother told her that. But he had too good a memory for the days of the Republic—a hundred years ago. He spoke of the Republic as if it were still here. Was he not one of a great Republican family and his blood far better than that of the Emperor? Of course no emperor would stand for such a man. But Mother had said she must be proud of Father.

There was Marcus, too, greeting all the guests. He wore a pure white toga and his hair was still wet and glistening from the comb. Lavinia had never realized that Marcus was beautiful, but he was beautiful. So handsome and getting tall, too. Only last week he had assumed the *toga virilis*. Rome now counted him a man. Fifteen was somewhat young for this important change. But, of course, Father wanted Marcus to assume the toga in the Roman Forum. The ceremony would not seem real if performed elsewhere. Marcus would go on and on being a man. But Lavinia would not see him when he was a man. Perhaps she would never see him after this day. No, no, she must not look at Marcus any more for the tears were stinging her eyes and her throat felt strange and lumpy.

She looked down at her hand on which was Decimus' ring. Any moment now Decimus would come. Any moment! She watched the front door with fixed eyes. Curious how long the time seemed. Oh, there was Rullianus, Decimus' father. She had seen him at the betrothal. He would be *her* father now for she would belong to his gens. And there was Decimus' mother, Paula, stout and gentle looking. How strange to think that Paula was her mother and not Aurelia any longer. But all was strange this morning—very strange. Everything that happened seemed clear and distinct, almost as if Lavinia could see it beforehand.

Now Paula came and kissed her. "Decimus will be here in a moment," she said merrily. "He is in his room dressing. Ah, these bridegrooms! They must deck themselves to the limit on their wedding mornings, and Decimus is always slow at dressing."

"What a peculiar girl," Paula was thinking. "I never saw an expression like that on any bride's face."

The slaves were waiting at the back of the atrium with the steaming dishes in their hands fresh from the kitchen. The banquet would begin. More moments. More moments. Lavinia never thought she would want to see Decimus. But she longed for him to come and the shock be over. The guests were talking and laughing, but gradually they did not talk so much nor laugh any more and they, too, began glancing toward the door.

It was full day now. A ray of sunshine was creeping along the outer edge of the roof hole. The sun must be pretty high. She saw Rullianus send off a slave hastily. He looked worried.

"There's been some accident," he muttered. "Why, even last night my son was perfectly ready."

Suddenly upon the silence came a clatter of hoofs in the street. How dared a man ride horse in the Roman streets in broad daylight? The hoofs stopped with loud stamping and a young Roman pushed by the porter into the room. His face was red as if he had drunk much wine.

"I have a message from Decimus," he said in a loud voice, "a message to his father. He wished me to state that he will not marry Lavinia Claudia. He has gone to Spain."

For a second the whole roomful were still as death, then Rullianus' angry voice, "By the gods! Go after him, Lucius! Leon!" he called to his slaves.

"There is no use, Rullianus," said the young Roman. "The ship sailed at midnight."

"But," cried out Paula, "he was in his room, dressing, this morning."

"My brother looks a lot like Decimus by torchlight," sneered Decimus' friend. "And you, after all, did not enter the room. The marriage is off."

Favonius turned red to the roots of his hair.

"This offense was intended!" he burst out. "This offense was intended."

They were all so angry—so frustrated—so bewildered—that no one noticed the little bride whom it concerned most of all. But now above the confusion was a piercing curious cry and Lavinia stretched both her childish arms out toward her mother.

"I'm going with you, I'm going with—I'm going with you."

She began to laugh loudly, then all of a sudden she was sobbing and crying. Aurelia ran from her place on the other side of the table and caught Lavinia in her arms.

"Be quiet, dearest, be quiet," she pleaded. Aurelia lifted her, almost carrying her from the room. But Lavinia couldn't be quiet. If she stopped sobbing it was only to laugh again. If she stopped laughing she was to say over and over, "I am going with you, I'm going with you."

Aurelia hurried to her own bedroom—laid Lavinia on the bed. Ino brought wine from the banquet table and made Lavinia drink it. Paula stood by the bed crying almost like Lavinia herself.

"The poor little bride! What an insult! Decimus has been cruel but never so cruel as this. Oh, Aurelia, what can we do to make up for this? What can we do? What is poor, dear Lavinia saying?"

"She doesn't know what she is saying," Aurelia answered hurriedly. "She is beside herself. She will soon be quiet. Ino, hold her while I go to her father."

Aurelia was terrified lest Claudius do some dreadful thing,

say some unforgivable word. She and Paula came again into the buzzing atrium.

Rullianus was talking in a commanding voice.

"Favonius, you can say what you will but this insult was never intended. I hereby disown my son. He has disgraced me over and over again and now he has defied me. The patrimony which was to be his I hereby give to your daughter whom he has so greatly wronged. Is there anything else I can do to wipe out the disgrace of Decimus?" Favonius suddenly changed. Severe and haughty he was yet he knew sincerity when he saw it. He spoke now in the clear voice the Claudians used in oratory.

"It is not for me to distrust the word of a friend in my own house. What has happened has happened." He stopped silent, looked about the assembly.

"Ye are my guests," he said. "Here is a banquet spread; let us pour wine to the gods and begin."

CHAPTER THREE

ALL THE GUESTS as they feasted that morning kept thinking with pity of the bride who, of course, did not appear again. Even Aurelia thought that Lavinia would be heartbroken at such humiliation. But as for Lavinia, whatever the hurt, it was completely swallowed up and lost in the joy of escape. She was bird free; she was winged! She was to be forever with the dear familiar ones she loved. She was not to be the property of the cruel, unknown Decimus. Decimus was gone—gone—gone!

During the long hours of the banquet, whenever Aurelia could get away to go to her daughter she would find her lying on the bed, her arms spread, her eyes shining, her cheeks aglow.

"Mother, I am going with you," she would repeat.

"Yes, dear."

"Mother, I am going with Marcus."

"Yes, dear."

"Mother, I am going with Father."

"Yes, darling, I know."

"Mother, I am going to Britain."

It was like a song which she must sing out of her heart with all the repetitions of a song. Not until evening, all the guests gone and the house quiet, did Lavinia finally go to sleep.

In the days that followed her joyousness seemed to reach to the land to which they were bound.

"Britannia," Lavinia would say softly to herself. "Britannia—Britannia."

All would be safe there. Never in Britannia would she be asked to marry a man like Decimus. Never would there be the cruel Emperor nor the secret dangers of which even Father was afraid. In Britannia she could stay a girl for years and years.

"Where is Britannia?" she asked.

"Dear, it is far away—on the very edge of the world," said Aurelia sadly. "It is an island, so I am told."

On the edge of the world! Why, then, beyond it would be the Deep Gulf of Nothingness, filled with stars and clouds. Of course the world was flat and Britannia was on the edge. Wonderful, wonderful to see that! Lavinia was not afraid. She had conquered her fear of Decimus and with it had gone all the foul ghosts of fear that had ever beset her.

Rome, which she had loved, seemed dark and unhappy in comparison. One evening when no one was looking she went to the door of the house and kissed the worn stone doorpost by which the Claudians had passed in and out, in and out for three hundred years.

"I am glad you are going to disappear," she said softly. "I am glad no one will see you when we are gone. You will never be lonely for us. You are ours, ours."

It seemed, strangely, for a moment that she could take the doorposts with her, the whole house and the garden, invisible in her heart.

As she came back into the house she found herself seeing the space of it intensely so she could never forget it. The quiet stone-paved atrium with its pool reflecting the sky, its faint, ancient wall paintings, the alae or wing rooms that spread either side like the beams of a cross—the tablinium at the back with the curtains spread apart. Later eyes would have thought it looked like a church but to Lavinia it was only home and the essence of home.

Suddenly she was aware of a sound of weeping—such miserable, choked weeping. She hurried through the tablinium to the garden. There under a laurel was Ino, her form bent over, her face covered.

"Ino, Ino, what is the matter?" Lavinia pulled away the gnarled old hands from the slave's face. "Why are you crying so?"

"Oh, little mistress—but I cannot tell you."

"You must must tell me. Is anybody hurt or ill?"

"No, no, it is only my own troubles. They mean nothing to you."

"But they would. What are your troubles, Ino?"

In her new and tender mood Lavinia felt that even a slave must not be weeping. Besides, she loved Ino. She had never known a time when Ino had not served and helped her.

"Ye could not mend them, little mistress."

"Don't be foolish, Ino. How do you know I can't mend them? Tell me—it is my command."

"Well, then, little mistress, it's my son. I must leave him and never see him again."

"Your son?"

Lavinia knew that Ino had a son. But she had quite forgotten it. Ino's relationships were so unimportant save that one of being maid in the Favonius family. Ino's son, yes, he made images. Ino used to tell her about him long ago and how some dreadful people called Christians tried to spoil his business. These Christians would not buy images themselves and they tried to prevent others from buying. Also, they were known to feast in dark caves on the blood of little children, and if Lavinia would not go to sleep like a good child when Ino put her to bed, the Christians would come and get her. Lavinia shuddered as the memory came back clear and full of dread. For a long while now she had not had that vivid dream—the Christians crawling out from under her bed, grinning at her with wide open mouths, snatching at her like harpies.

She was not afraid now. But she was glad there would be no Christians in Britannia. Ah, that was too far away for them. Far away and safe.

Ino, lifting her head, saw that her little mistress had forgotten her. At this the sobs suddenly got the better of Ino. They shook her old frame. They were heartbroken and aloud. They shook Lavinia out of her dream.

"Oh, Ino, Ino, I am so sorry. I didn't know that you—"

She stopped. She was ashamed of what she was about to say, that she did not know Ino could love her son. Pity, that feeling so unaccustomed to the Roman, took hold of Lavinia. She was almost angry for she saw no way out.

"Tell me about him, Ino. Oh, I don't want you to be sad. I don't want you to cry."

The new note in her little mistress's voice astonished Ino. She began to tell her story, hardly knowing that she did so.

"Cleon—you'll hardly remember him, little mistress. Master sold him before you were born—to Publius Mero, him who lives at the bottom of this street. He allowed my

Cleon to work in his spare time, making little images of wood and stone, and Cleon sold them. Oh, so smart was my Cleon. At last he had made enough to buy his freedom. He is a freedman now and he has a good business with his images and ornaments. Almost he has enough to buy his wife and two children. But, oh, little mistress, he says he will buy me first and wait for his wife. And he must not. He must not. His wife would hate me. I'd hate myself, being free in her stead—old and useless."

"You're not useless—not useless," cried out Lavinia. She was hurt by this tale. There was no help. It was dreadful. Ino's grief would haunt her. It was bad enough for Mother to have to leave all her family—for Father to be burdened with so much sorrow, and now this!

"I won't let him buy you," she said helplessly.

"Oh, little mistress—I've settled that already. He's angry with me, is Cleon."

A look of shame and plotting came over Ino's face. A sly look. She took Lavinia's hand and kissed it.

"There *is* a way, little mistress," she whispered.

"A way!" Lavinia repeated.

"Yes—yes." Ino lost her breath. It was a dreadful thing she was proposing. What would little mistress do?

"Yes, little mistress. If—if—Master gave me—my freedom—I could stay in Rome. I'm not much good—not much more use to ye all, I am not—" She fell on her knees, clasping Lavinia about her knees.

For a moment Lavinia was indeed horrified. The ingratitude after all these years of being in the house! Ino! Wanting to be free of them all! Not to belong to them. Then again that queer understanding came over Lavinia.

"I'm going to ask Father," she said.

23

"Oh no, no—he'll whip me."

"I'll beg him not to. We'll have to take the chance—yes."

She stood up straight, trying to plan. "Go to my room, Ino. He'll be home soon," she said.

She went to the front door and waited just inside. More than once her courage failed her. Suppose Father were angry and made a scene. Suppose he should whip Ino—poor old Ino who never had been struck in Lavinia's memory of her. Every once in a while Lavinia could hear a gulp of weeping from Ino—but somehow this made her more determined.

Now came Father's footsteps in the street—many footsteps. She hoped friends were not with him. No, only the slaves and Marcus. He was here. She seized his hand.

"Father, I want to ask you something. Wait a moment, Father."

Favonius was struck with the earnestness in her face.

"Well, well, hurry up about it; I have no time to lose."

(Yes, he was impatient, and very busy.)

"I want to ask you—"

"Whatever is the matter with you, Lavinia? I have a thousand things to do!"

"It's about Ino. I want you to give her her freedom. So she won't have to go with us. She is old and every day she is more helpless—and—she'd only be a burden—and—" Lavinia was talking very fast.

"Ino's freedom! By Pollux, I didn't think you had that much sense. I've been wanting to propose it to your mother but she's so sentimental about the old slaves. If we take Ino she'll like as not die on the way."

"Yes—yes, Father, I'm sure she would," said Lavinia breathlessly. This answer was a surprise.

"On the other hand, she may die in poverty on the streets

of Rome—you must think of that."

"Oh no, Father. Her son Cleon will take care of her."

"Her son? Now how do you know that, young lady?"

"Ino told me."

"Has Ino asked for her freedom?"

"No, Father, I just thought of it."

"No, you did not. Daughter, you are a poor liar. Bring Ino to me."

"Oh, please, please, don't whip her."

"Of course not, little fool. Have I ever whipped her?" demanded Favonius. "I shall go forward with it, however, before your mother hears of it. Marcus"—he turned to his son—"go quickly to Publius Mero and ask him to come here this afternoon. And to bring" (he named Rullianus and four other friends) "as witnesses for a manumission."

It was a solemn moment. In the cool of the afternoon came the important dignified friends of Favonius Claudius. Publius Mero was praetor—that made the manumission legal and certain. With him came his lictor, bearing the tall, heavy insignia of Mero's office. They stood in the atrium. Tears streamed down Aurelia's cheeks. If Ino had been a blood relation, Aurelia could hardly have felt her more near. She had been in the house when Aurelia had come, a timid bride. Ino, more than anyone, had comforted her, and it was Ino who understood the care of the babies. Aurelia was hurt that Ino wanted to part from them.

As for Ino herself—she trembled and quivered so that Lavinia had to keep her arm close about her and help her stand. Cleon was there for of course he had heard. Slaves and freedmen hear everything. It was he who brought the *pillius*—his own "liberty cap"—which was always put on the head of the slave at the moment of freedom.

Lavinia pushed Ino forward, and Ino knelt on the pavement which for so many years she had traversed on countless errands.

The lictor advanced, lifting high a rod called *vindicta*. He laid hold of Ino's shoulder, pronouncing the words, "Hunc ego hominum, ex iure Quiritium liberum esse aio." Then he touched her with the rod and let go of her.

Now came Favonius. He also touched Ino with the rod. He lifted her to her feet, held her hand, turned her about, and with a flourish let her go—pronouncing her free. He took the "liberty cap" from Cleon and put it on her head.

Lavinia was astonished to find tears coursing down her own cheeks. She stepped forward and kissed Ino as if she had been a bride.

What an odd look in Ino's eyes! She had never known her to look like that—a proud, aloof look such as Favonius himself might wear. She was muttering to herself, "I never thought I'd be free. Why, I am Greek again—an Arcadian."

She was funny, was Ino in the high felt hat. Marcus giggled aloud. But Lavinia did not want to laugh. Her heart was speaking of the dearness of Ino, the nearness of Ino who now would never be near again.

Cleon took his mother's hand, bowed low before Favonius with whispered and most humble thanks. Aurelia kissed Ino, but the old slave seemed almost unaware. Then Cleon, carrying the heavy bundle of things they had given Ino, led her out the door.

That night for the first time in her life Lavinia was waited upon and undressed by a young house slave. She had not known how strange and lonely this would seem.

CHAPTER FOUR

T FIRST the relief of Lavinia's going had been so great for Aurelia it had quite taken away all the sadness of departure. But there were her sisters, her brother, her aged mother, her aunt Aurelia whom surely she would never see again. The sadness could not but steal back upon her heart like a cold east wind. And Aurelia did not share Lavinia's hopefulness about the new land. She even demeaned herself to do something no Roman lady should do. She sent for a slave whom her tiring woman knew—a man who had been to Britain. He came to the door and she asked him questions.

"Oh, it's a grand land, *domina*. A pretty land as pretty as any ye may see!"

She gave him a sesterce. "Now tell me the truth," she demanded, "and I'll give you more."

The man's face changed.

"Well, then, *domina*, 'tis a horrid land and that's the truth. Never was I so glad as when my master brought me away from it."

"Is it cold?" she questioned.

"Cold! Oh, *domina,* ye don't know the meanin' o' cold till ye get there. Frost and fallin' snow thick an' heavy as sand by the sea. And it's a godless land. How do I know that? Because there's no day there."

"No day!" repeated Aurelia. "Oh, now you are lying in the other direction. Gods help me."

"No, *domina.* I'm not not lyin'. The sun, it doesn't get up till nigh onto noon and it's down again by the tenth hour o' the day. An even shinin', its light is thin an' watery—and then there's the little people."

"The little people. What do you mean by that?"

The man held his palm about a foot above the ground.

"Little people about *that* tall, *domina.* They lives in the woods an' on the cold, cold mountain tops, by the old cairns of stone that the giants put there. Some says they're green color. Some says—but all folk says they're cold like lizards. Ye unnerstand they're not human—the little people."

Aurelia listened, fascinated. Not ready to believe in the darkness of Britain, she did more than believe in these wood spirits. Every land had its own.

"Have you seen them?" she inquired.

"No, *domina,* I haven't. Romans and foreign people don't see 'em much. But the Brythons sees 'em often and often. Sometimes the little people is good to ye and sometimes— oh, dreadful, mischievous and harmful, leadin' ye astray in the swamps, an' stealin' the senses out o' little babies—yes, they do. And maybe takin' off the baby itself an' puttin' their own queerlike baby in its place."

It was all so detailed, so particular. Aurelia shuddered.

"Oh, I wish I had not asked you!" she said, giving him more money. "Go away, go away."

Even so, Aurelia would not damp Lavinia's ardor. Let her

think the land beautiful and kind. Indeed her daughter's hopefulness was all that kept up Aurelia's heart in these tragic days.

Then suddenly, as suddenly as the wedding day, came the day of departure, a clap of thunder in the arch of time. Incredibly all was ready to the last detail. All furniture packed or disposed of. All the clothes bound up in heavy cloth or in baskets and piled in the atrium. Dawn not yet come, yet everybody hurrying through the dimly lighted rooms. Torches flaring, lamps smelling of oil. "Where is the wine basket?" "Where the food baskets?" "Don't forget the fresh onions and parsley." "We can't get that on the road!" "Oh, if it were only not so cold! The braziers are all packed and no time anyway to light a fire."

The priests come with the report of auspices. Now the family is sacrificing before the little household altar.

For the last time.

Not anyone standing there in the silence will ever forget it. Not Marcus to whom these moments mark the border line between child and manhood. Not Favonius Claudius who will always remember with regret. Not Aurelia to whom it is a heartbreak. Not Lavinia to whom it is love and preciousness and wonder.

They pour wine on the floor.

Now the most trusted slaves come forward. They lift out the images one by one and put them in the tiny traveling altar which is like a treasure chest, the dancing skirted boy who lifts high the cup of libation, the tiny solemn Vesta, the silver vessels of sacrifice. Did the little bearded man look back? Lavinia thought so. Why would he not after three hundred years? She felt specially safe now that the little man was going too.

At the door was a litter for Father and Marcus, a litter for Lavinia and her mother. Strong Cappadocian slaves carried them, for horses were allowed in few streets of Rome and even in them never for the first ten hours of the day. Slave-drawn carts carried the baggage.

Other slaves walked. Still others carried torches. For the streets of Rome were not lighted. Nobody felt anything now. In a sort of numbness they passed the sleeping houses down the hill where the temples of the Forum were just opening and the shivering slaves stumbling about on errands.

"Aurelia," called Favonius Claudius, a solemn note in his voice.

Aurelia knew what he meant. She opened the curtains of the litter and looked out. There was the "golden milestone" of Rome. The stone faced with bronze from which all the miles in the world were measured. Now came the less important streets, turning, twisting, narrow. But to Favonius every turn was dear, every corner was important. Now the shopkeepers were taking down the fronts of the shops. The torches gave them momentary flashes of pots—bread—sweetmeats—images—which were set out on the counters for sale.

Suddenly they were at the river and crossing the Pons Aemilius, a bridge spanning the Tiber, and could see the thrice-sacred island of Esculapius where people went to be cured of diseases. On the other side they were in the low river plain. The river mists penetrated the litters, very chill. But soon they began to climb the steep, steep slopes of the Janiculum.

Day was dimly breaking when they reached the Porta Aurelia.

"It is your same name, Mother," whispered Lavinia.

"Maybe that will bring you good luck."

"It is the Fates," responded her mother.

Perhaps in all Rome there was not a gate more beautiful for situation than this. For it stood like an impregnable fortress on the height of the Janiculum. On either side the city wall serpentined down the hill, and away below and in front stretched the plains to Ostia. In the rear were the roofs and templed hills of Rome.

Important! What is more important than a city gate at dawn—a symbol of all beginnings, a rush of life like a stream breaking through a dam? The guards had just opened the huge double doors and the smaller doors for foot passengers. Market men with their carts and donkeys (the only vehicles allowed in Rome by day) pushed in, bumping each other, swearing as a donkey's load was knocked askew. The guard itself was changing, the new soldiers marching to their place—with clang of armor and glitter of shields. Foot passengers crowded under the smaller arches, some of them running. Others were trying to get out of the city as was the Claudian party.

Aurelia crouched close in the curtains but Lavinia peeped through a tiny slit. At last they were beyond the gate. Good! They would have to change. For here they were to take the horse-drawn vehicles which Claudius had purchased for the journey.

As Aurelia and Lavinia came out of the parted curtains, they were met and embraced by Aurelia's mother and sisters. What a crowd! Even Aunt Aurelia was there, causing a little stir among the people for a Vestal was always important. Who would have thought so many would come out to bid them good-by?

There were Marcus' friends, four young men. They were

hiring a *cisium,* one of the small carriages at the gate, to go a half day's journey with Marcus. There was Aemilia, Lavinia's cousin, who was her special friend in all the family. Of course neither Aemilia nor the aunts could go part way. They must say good-by here and now.

And there were friends of Favonius greeting him, clasping his hand. Cousins of the family, an aged uncle, fellow officers of his legion who had been with him on campaigns.

"We'll be seeing you again in Rome, Favonius, never fear," they said.

But their looks belied their words. It was no small thing to incur the displeasure of the Emperor and be sent to a distant province. It was a dangerous post to which Claudius was going.

There was Rullianus. Lavinia's heart leaped with fear. Suppose Rullianus had got Decimus back! Suppose even now he would take her! The day went black and bleak for Lavinia. But Rullianus was not looking at her. He had brought a parting gift to Favonius Claudius. He was handing him a large silver traveling cup. Favonius was touched. His face flushed painfully. He thanked Rullianus and passed the cup about to all his friends, then brought it over to Aurelia.

It was a tall cup shaped like an ornamental milestone and was inscribed with the principle stations on the way: Alsium, Pisae, Genua, Forum Julii, Nemausis, Lugudunum. Aurelia's heart sank. These last she knew were in Gaul. Lavinia noted each one as if it were a jewel. This and this and this would Lavinia see with her own eyes.

They were no small company of travelers. First came the two strong Cappadocian slaves who had carried the litter, driving now a covered cart with Favonius' special treasure and the *lares* and *penates* of the home altar. They were armed. Then the carriage for Favonius and Marcus; near this a powerful horse ridden by Favonius. For though Romans did not usually travel on horseback, Favonius, accustomed to long campaigns in foreign lands, preferred it. Then came the *raeda* in which Aurelia and Lavinia were already seated. Then wagons with their special slaves. More than twenty slaves were walking, some driving the laden carts, some the pack mules.

Last of all came a company of thirty armed legionaries who were being sent to Britain to join one of the legions. These were a needed protection in the farther portions of the journey. Hadrian himself was now absent from Rome; the traveling Emperor he was called. He knew nothing of this favor to Favonius. But it had been arranged by those who dared to do so.

As they went down the hill they were a long procession in the new golden day. From the gate on the hilltop came the voices, "*Vale, vale, vale,*" as the friends called their good-bys. Ever fainter the sound as the company moved onward, onward, leaving the Eternal City.

Among them all was only one who did not leave it with regret and even sorrow. Only one who was strangely looking forward.

So began the long journey to Britain.

CHAPTER FIVE

"LOOK, MOTHER. Oh, Mother—look!"

Through the long weeks that followed Aurelia was to hear this over and over again. Always the ringing enthusiasm. Always the delight until Aurelia, for all her sadness, had to catch a sense of outward going. But Aurelia heard it first at Alsium where the Via Aurelia meets the sea.

Lavinia herself parted the curtains of the *raeda*. At first she could not speak at all, then she said under her breath:

"I didn't know it was so big. How can it meet the sky like that? How blue. How blue. Mother, it's like the sapphires in that necklace of Aunt Julia's. Do you suppose if I dipped some up in a cup it would be full of sapphires?"

"No, daughter, of course not. It would be just plain water, except, of course, very salt. Surely you are not so ignorant. But then you were so little when we made our visits to the villas."

"Only Rome," said Lavinia, "that's all I remember."

"Only Rome! Ah, that should be enough," thought Aurelia.

Straight ahead—ruler straight—ran the North Road—its well-fitted large stones deeply rutted with the thousands of wheels that came daily to and from Rome. The road surface was slightly arched to drain off the rain. At one side was the foot pavement. All was built up from the low ground like a causeway. Such a road! And it was Rome's proud boast that she flung them like this, forth from her nine gates throughout all the countries of the world. Even Rome did not know they were so strong and well made that they would outlast Rome herself by a thousand years.

Now the travelers were passing one of the tall ornamental milestones inscribed with mottoes.

Aurelia, reading it, felt her heart constrict with pain. "So many miles from Rome," she thought, "and I'll never see even this milestone again."

Marcus and his friends, crowded in their hired *cisium*, were driving alongside.

Lavinia could hear them chatting.

"Too bad, old fellow, you had to miss the games today," said one.

"Well, you're missing them too," responded Marcus politely.

"All for the love of you," laughed a third friend.

"Sorry you had to miss them yesterday too."

"Couldn't get away," said Marcus gloomily. "The horrid packing and getting ready."

"It was grand," went on the third boy. "The big circus was so crowded it looked like a frothy sea. Ten gladiators were killed one right after the other—fighting against net and tridant. Then came the eleventh. By Pollux, he was a giant and black as ebony. I never saw such a battle as he put up. And the arena all slippery with blood too. The people went wild."

"I heard 'em," put in Marcus eagerly. "I heard 'em at home."

"Gods! you could have heard 'em beyond the walls!" By this time two boys were talking at once with the third interrupting.

"He fought and fought—he killed one antagonist after another."

"Did they free him?" demanded Marcus.

"Yes—yes, they did just that. He asked for reward and they bellowed."

" 'Free! Free! Free!' But what do you think?—after they freed him, he was walking off and he suddenly fell down and died. He'd fought the whole last fight with a mortal wound."

"By Hercules—that was an experience."

Favonius drove his horse alongside so as to join in the talk. He was full of regret that Marcus would no longer attend the games at Rome. Yet more regretful for himself. Were not the games a warlike pleasure, training the Roman to grim sights and sounds? But the games were also a great political force.

The Emperor himself feared their factions. Favonius belonged to one faction. Perhaps that was not a little of the cause why the Emperor was getting rid of him.

When they had passed Alsium the boys had to turn back to Rome, a last good-by which solemnized even their young spirits. Marcus was quite blue for an hour. After Alsium the Via Aurelia was not so straight. It curved inward and outward, following the gracious sculpture of the sea. This was not what the Roman builders wished, for they were for swiftness and practicality every time. But here they could not help it, so created beauty, all unintending.

Some distance inland were gentle hills turning golden against the western light. Close to the road were olive orchards in new leaf—the gray verdure tender but lusty, all in good condition fostered by the security of the Roman government. This was Etruria, the ancient land whose mysterious people joined long ago with the Romans and gave them a fierceness that was to last through all their common history. Sometimes the travelers saw old Etruscan tombs overgrown with meadow grass.

That night they stayed at a friend's villa. Lavinia had often stayed overnight with her cousin Aemilia, but this experience outside Rome was new to her. The strange rooms, the strange slaves, the smell of the sea, and as night deepened, the eternal sound of the sea. She could hardly sleep for listening to it and wondering about the sea.

All next day the travelers moved in a region of pine forests. And as the days of travel multiplied these grew more dense. In spite of the constant traffic of the road, the mood of the pine forest became regnant, filling the air with scent and the scene with a certain quiet solemnity. On the western side of the road the beaches widened until they were broad pavements of white bordering the sea. From any height the beach could be seen for miles, curving to the inlets, pushing out with the capes into the sunny sea.

The second night was spent at Punicum in another villa, the third in the hill villa of a stranger in Aquae Tauri. At Craviscae they were forced to stop at an inn which was in the nature of a calamity. Inns were of the worst. But to Lavinia even its discomforts were tasted as adventure. All, all the journeying was a growing delight, a music that approached a climax in slow rhythmic strides.

But to Aurelia it was increasing weariness. Aurelia had never been strong and these hours of jolting tired her. No Roman vehicles had springs, and even a multitude of cushions could not protect an aching back. Favonius noted her weariness with alarm.

"But the journey has hardly begun," he said, riding vigorously along by her *raeda*. It seemed incredible that his wife should already be tired.

He galloped away on some errand but soon came back again. The mind of Favonius was a wide realm of pride, endurance, unbending purpose, cruelty and Roman virtue. The one corner of it reserved for affection belonged to Aurelia. Indeed, his chief grief in leaving Rome was the exiling of Aurelia from her home.

"Are you still tired?" he queried fifteen minutes later.

Aurelia laughed at him.

"It still jolts," she said. "But surely I'll get hardened to it. It is the long, long hours of monotony!"

Lavinia caught her breath. How could Mother say that when the pine forests had come and the sea and the open sunshine and the blue sky?

Favonius frowned. Presently he said:

"Would it help if I brought Angelion to tell stories?"

"Perhaps so," said Aurelia.

Angelion was a slave whom they had bought three years ago. Favonius had run across him in the market selling cheap because he was ill. But Favonius saw his worth and trusted to Aurelia's medical skill. Angelion had begun to improve at once, a sensitive Greek suffering from the abuse of a foolish master and appreciating to the full the kindness and the serene life of the Claudian household.

Soon he was put to use entertaining guests at feasts. Talented and quick, he gave a performance which became famous among the set in which the Claudians moved. Favonius Claudius could not have afforded such a fine slave except by the happy chance of rescuing him at the sale.

Now Angelion came and walked beside the litter in the sunshine.

"What will you have, *domina*?" he said respectfully as he easily kept pace with the horses of the *raeda*.

"What about that play you gave when Pliny spent the evening with us and was so delighted."

"That was the *Ion of Euripides*. I did not give it all, *domina*."

"Give it all now. There is time and to spare."

Lavinia was delighted. First because now she need not keep begging Mother to open the curtains, secondly because she loved stories and had always been considered too young to come to the feasts. She thought of Angelion as being almost old. He was about thirty. But she could not fail to note his beauty. He was a Dorian. That is, his hair was brown instead of black, his eyes hazel. He was stockily built but exceedingly graceful, a gracefulness born of strength, as if the centuries of athletics of his ancestors still persisted in spite of slavery. The brown tunic did not look slave-like upon him. Very alert, he was quick to hear, quick to respond. He gestured as he talked and smiled often. He loved Aurelia for what she had done for him. He loved the poetry he was reciting. Soon Lavinia was lost even to the beauty about her, being translated to Delphi with its beetling crags, its Shining Rocks, its multitude of temples and treasures.

"Good, good," applauded Aurelia. "Angelion, you make me feel as if I were there in Delphi."

"I *am* there, *domina*," he answered. "I have always been there."

"What do you mean? You were born to Vegellius' house; he was your master—you have said so often."

"Yes, *domina*—my body—but not my spirit. It was my grandfather who was snatched away from Delphi during a

Roman raid. But he was a priest. Always from father to son we have told each other of our Delphi. We do not forget."

Aurelia did not like the emotional ring of his voice—the turn that the talk had taken.

"Proceed, Angelion," she said, though not unkindly.

Angelion saw the picture so intensely that his imagination flashed over to Lavinia. Afterward she could hardly believe that she had not seen the white flock fluttering down from the air to sip the poisoned wine from the road. They fell dead—all the doves—and with their innocent sacrifice saved the life of Ion.

"Bravo! bravo!" Lavinia shouted.

Oh, lovely to be going forward bodily into a new world while her young spirit was advancing into a wonderland of poetry.

The play took only an hour, for all Greek plays were short. Next day Angelion came again, for it was plain that the recital had greatly helped Aurelia.

After that each day he recited, sometimes striding along in the rain, sometimes in the bitter wind which suddenly blew from the north. All weathers seemed alike to him when he was once in his realm of poetry.

They reached Pisae at the end of two weeks. Pisae was then only two miles from the sea at the confluence of two muddy little rivers. It was Pisa without its Leaning Tower, its echoing Baptistry, its Field of Miracles. The town was hundreds of years old. Like all the towns on the coast it was a "little Rome," the same Forum, the same temple, basilica and baths, the same circus for games. Only Pisae was a bigger and more important "little Rome" than the others and the baths here, a short distance from the town, had a natural warm spring and mineral water. Favonius was delighted for

Aurelia to take the baths, and to both of them it was a great refreshment. Lavinia, too, enjoyed the baths but after two days was already impatient to go onward.

Lavinia was one of those rare persons, exceedingly rare in Rome, to whom the world is a vast storehouse of treasure and surprise. One of those who will undergo any hardship to behold beauties afar. Of course, Lavinia did not know this. In the four walls of the house on the Clivus Victoriae, it did not occur to her that she would ever see beyond the confines of her city. The last of their villas had been lost to Favonius when she was a baby. They did not go forth into the country as did their richer neighbors. The wish in Lavinia's heart was so deep down she did not know it existed.

But with the first knowledge that she was going to Britain this longing began to awake like a hibernating animal after winter sleep. She was excited as one who expects good news. Such people are born to adventure because adventure is within them. She was impatient to be going onward to Britain.

CHAPTER SIX

UT THE third morning as she and her mother with their slaves passed through the market she saw something which made her forget even Britain. For there, stamping and restless, was a herd of Celtic ponies which had been brought from the north. They were queer beasts. They still had their winter coats of long hair, longer than a goat's, and a beard under their lower jaw. Some of them were large and more horselike and of pure white. These, so said the dealer, had come from the forest of Britain. Favonius and Marcus were fascinated with them. They were going from one to another deciding which to buy. Marcus was to have one and Claudius was buying several others. They did not notice that Lavinia had broken away from her mother's party and run to Marcus.

"Oh, Marcus, are you really going to have a pony of your own?" she whispered.

"Yes—this little devil. Isn't he strong? I'll bet you he could climb a mountain like a goat, and he's swift too."

"His hair is like a goat's," commented Lavinia, lovingly stroking him.

"Careful, sister," warned Marcus. "The dealer says they bite as quick as wolves do."

"He won't bite me," said Lavinia. "Oh, Marcus, if I could have one, I think I would die of joy."

"That's a silly thing to say."

"Yes," agreed Lavinia, laughing. "Because I wouldn't die. I'd ride him."

"You ride! A girl!"

"Well, I could, if I wore just my tunic and *cucullus*. That would hide me so no one would know I was a girl."

Suddenly Marcus' mood changed.

"By Pollux," he said, "I wish you could have a pony. I'm going to ride by myself but I'm tired of going along without Titus and Verrus and Lucius. Why, we were somewhere in Rome together every day."

(They were the boys who had driven to Alsium with Marcus.)

"And, by Hera, I've been riding with old Icinus for three days now. That's a bore."

"With Icinus," repeated Lavinia, amazed that her father should give a seat in the *raeda* to a slave.

"Yes, he's gone lame and sick too. Father values him because he speaks several languages of Britannia—and came from there as a young man. He'll be no end of help to us if he ever gets there alive."

Just here came Favonius.

"Well, son," he said pleasantly, "have you picked out a pony to your liking?"

"Yes, this one," Marcus replied. "The dealer says he's fierce at times but he's got spirit and go."

"Try him," said Favonius.

So the dealer strapped a thick blanket about the horse

and adjusted the bridle. Marcus sprang on him and was off like the wind down one of the streets of Pisae. He came back glowing and sprang to the ground.

"This is the one!" he exulted.

The dealer who had overheard the conversation with Lavinia now brought forward a large white pony.

"How about this also?" he said. "This little mare came from the forests of Britannia. She must have been somebody's pet. As gentle as a lamb. Not like the others."

"My son isn't buying a lamb," asserted Favonius.

"But, master, maybe your daughter would."

Claudius had not even seen Lavinia standing there. His mind was wholly upon Marcus.

"What foolish talk is this?" he demanded. "Lavinia, why aren't you with your mother?"

"I saw Marcus and I was talking with him. I'll—I'll go now."

Of course any hope of a pony died out of Lavinia's heart. But Marcus seemed suddenly to wake up.

"Father, it was my idea, too—not just Lavinia's. I wish she could ride with me."

"Marcus, are you crazy?"

"Yes, just about," said Marcus crossly. "Three days in old Icinus' company. And before that not a soul to talk to the whole way."

"But surely you don't want your sister seen riding horseback on the open road."

"No one will see her. She'll wear her big cloak. I'll take care of her. Lavinia is good company. In the cloak she'll look just like a boy."

Favonius was eager for Marcus to go hopefully to Britain. For Marcus there might be a career in the far-off land. Besides—for days Favonius had been wishing to have Lavinia's seat in the *raeda* with Aurelia. He wanted to see how Aurelia was getting along. He wanted her company. To Lavinia's amazement he began to hesitate.

"Are you sure you can take good care of her? Will you and Trogus teach her to ride?"

"Yes, yes—we'll teach her." Marcus' face flushed with pleasure.

"It's unheard of," grumbled Favonius Claudius. "A girl riding on the open road. We're getting to be barbarians because we are away from Rome."

But he had consented. He paid out the money to the dealer.

"Anyway, the little white horse is good property," he thought. "It need not always be used by Lavinia."

Lavinia hurried away to catch up with her mother. Indeed, the slave had already been sent back for her. She went to the baths—the warm, the hot, the cold. But she hardly felt them, she was so excited about the little white horse from Britain.

CHAPTER SEVEN

 EXT DAY they left Pisae. They had gone only a little way when Marcus came for Lavinia to ride.

"I never heard of such a thing," objected Aurelia. "A girl riding anywhere—especially on the public road. Are you sure Father wishes it?"

But there was Favonius too.

"Yes, yes," he interrupted. "It's high time I traveled with you, Aurelia. Let Marcus and Lavinia proceed together."

Favonius took the seat in the *raeda*. He had little to say. He was glad to find Aurelia stronger after the rest in Pisae. He was contented to be with her.

"Don't you want Angelion this morning?" he inquired. "It's pleasant to hear his voice rambling along, especially if he sings."

"Yes, send for him," agreed Aurelia.

Moments passed. A half-hour. Aurelia began to wonder at the delay. Now came the foreman of the slaves. He was pale and visibly trembling.

"Master," he said, "I've looked everywhere for Angelion. He's not among the household—nor the soldiers. Shall I go back for him to Pisae?"

"Tell me all of it," spoke Favonius Claudius flatly. For he knew by the man's fright there was more.

"I'd better go back to Pisae."

"Tell me what is the matter," thundered Favonius.

"Yes, O yes, master. They say they have not seen him for three days. I was busy with the horses and the gear and buying rations. I thought he was with the soldiers."

"You shall be whipped," declared Favonius. "The fellow has escaped beyond recall. There's a road"—he turned to Aurelia—"a road that starts from Pisae, across Italia to the sea. He's taken that. If I could catch him, I'd whip him until he'd never forget it."

"Then you'd lose your slave by another route," spoke Aurelia. "Angelion would not survive the disgrace."

"Surely you don't think he's excusable!"

"Of course not. But he's like that. He would die under the lash. That was all that was the matter with him when he came to us. Poor Angelion. Someone will capture him on the way. He'll only have a bad master in exchange for you."

"Yes—he'll be caught, that's certain," said Favonius. The thought gave him satisfaction. "Go get my horse, Puer."

The expression on Aurelia's face disturbed Favonius.

"You're grieved about Angelion," he said.

"No, I'm afraid you'll whip Puer for both. I hate these whippings. They make me ill."

"Puer is no weakling like Angelion."

"No. Puer can take it," she said with a sigh.

But somehow the satisfaction to be got out of whipping the slave died in Favonius. When Puer brought his horse later, he sent him off again, and Aurelia knew that Puer was probably to be spared. Also Puer knew who had saved him but, of course, he dared not show it even by a flick of the eyelash.

All morning Aurelia kept thinking of Angelion. Wicked and ungrateful as he had been, for so Aurelia judged him, she hoped he would win to Delphi. Was not she herself also an exile leaving Rome? Suppose she herself suddenly found a way to go back. How her heart would beat, how her hands would tremble with joy. Angelion was going home. Angelion would see his Shining Rocks. He would see the house of his fathers, the temples of his god.

Perhaps!

She dreaded to tell Lavinia. A slave was not a slave to a young mind. Lavinia would feel as if one of the family had run away.

Meanwhile Marcus led Lavinia back along the line of their party until they came to the horses and mules. Trogus had the new ponies ready.

"I tried to get this mare ready for little mistress," he announced. "But she's a funny-looking beast with her winter coat and all."

"I think she's beautiful," breathed Lavinia, too happy to talk very loud. She stroked the mare's nose and forehead.

"Aren't you beautiful?" she whispered to her. "Of course you're the most beautifullest horse in the world. Your hair's long but it's white and shines like silver. You're my silver pony. You are mine, mine."

The pony flicked her ears and lowered her nose against Lavinia's shoulder.

"See," she said foolishly. "She knows what I am saying."

Trogus strapped the blanket about the horse's middle and adjusted the bridle. There was no saddle nor stirrups.

"I wish I wasn't goin' to be the one to teach ye," he said

anxiously, as he lifted her up. She sat astride, the *currus* covering her completely, head and all.

"This here cloak will be the death o' ye," Trogus complained. "Hard enough for a girl to learn without wrappin' her all in cloak."

"Take it off," commanded Marcus who was now astride his pony and a little anxious himself. "There's nobody on the road back here. Even the soldiers have marched on ahead of us."

Trogus took off the cloak and gave it to the groom to carry.

"Now, little mistress, don't sit as if ye'd had a spear down yer back. Remember ye must make your pony obey ye, but ye must also obey her. Every move she makes must be your move too. You're a part o' her. See!"

Lavinia did see. Wasn't that the way Father rode? But she couldn't do it. No, she just kept bumping, bumping, like a bag of apples.

"I'm holdin' onto the halter," said Trogus, "and I'm doin' that for a week to come. Ye mustn't be afraid, like as if ye was ridin' alone."

But Lavinia was not afraid. Not the least in the world. She was not thinking of herself. But only of the pony. The absolute wonder of being astride a pony and out here in the open sunshine. Indeed, she was so happy and carefree that her rigidity began to depart.

"By Pollux, she's getting it," sang out Marcus. "She's sitting her horse. Let go the halter, Trogus."

But slave though he was, Trogus would not let go the halter. He had taught Marcus to ride and would allow no accidents. Lavinia insisted on nothing. Only trying to do whatever Trogus bade her or, better yet, too happy even to try.

The consequence was that she progressed beyond Marcus' fondest hopes.

"You're going to be a grand rider," Marcus told her as they hurried ahead in one of the wagons to overtake Aurelia. "By the time we reach Genua you'll really be riding with me. Trogus says you are a natural rider."

Marcus was happier than he had been any day on the road.

"I've named my pony Ventus, for he runs like the wind," added Marcus.

"I hope mine will run fast," said Lavinia wistfully.

"But she does. Trogus says that when yours gets a chance she runs like a *triga*. That's the three-horse chariot of the races. Of course you've never seen one. They just skim along reckless as the mischief."

"Oh, I'll call my pony Triga," cried out Lavinia. "That's just the right name for her."

Slowly the travelers were penetrating into the most beautiful coast in the world. At least if any other can boast of beauty this West Italian Coast can surely match it. The verdure was almost tropical—gray olive orchards in the valleys and even palms. Fruit trees frothed into white bloom and the slopes held prosperous vineyards.

The hills were mountains now, majestic overmastering, and they encroached even nearer to the sea, which received them with crashing breakers, and long lines of white foam ever rolling in from azure distances.

All her life Lavinia was to remember the scent of the blooming valleys mingled with the sea air of far distances. Blessed are those who travel at footpace and see all.

The White Isle

Chapter Eight

DON'T LIKE the looks o' them horses," said Trogus. "They dance too high on their toes. They had too good a rest at Genua an' that's the truth."

The travelers were a day's journey out of Genua. It was one of those hot spells of early spring which tries to persuade that summer has arrived, only to retire after a while into raw windy cold. It was now afternoon and the western sun beating on the cliffs increased the heat.

"Let Lavinia ride with me," begged Marcus. "The *raeda* is terribly hot and close."

So Lavinia climbed down from the curtained *raeda* and mounted her pony. The moment she was on its back, before she was settled or adjusted, Triga dashed off up the road. Lavinia had learned much of riding in these few weeks but she had never ridden so fast before. The rhythm of the gallop passing up into her body from the body of the horse delighted her. She seemed transformed into another creature, endowed with a swiftness and harmony of motion she had never known.

"Hold her back. Hold her back," came Marcus' voice, faint from far away and with such a note of alarm that Lavinia drew rein and talked to Triga. She slowed her down at last and Marcus came alongside.

"You mustn't go like that," he admonished her. "It's all very well for you to learn so well. But, after all, you're a new rider and you must remember it."

"Yes, but, oh, it was wonderful. If Triga could stand it, I'd like to go like that all the time."

Favonius, riding up to take his place by Aurelia, had looked at the performance with pure amazement.

"Why, she rides like a boy. I never knew it was within the power of a girl to do that—and especially Lavinia. She's always so stupid."

"Oh, Favonius—don't say that," pleaded Aurelia. "You don't know Lavinia."

"Don't know my own daughter after thirteen years!" laughed Favonius, forgetting all about it that moment.

On and on rode Marcus and Lavinia, far ahead of everybody. They were both perspiring in the close heat and both perfectly unconscious of it as young people are. Now the burning sun got clouded over and they were glad.

"By Pollux, it was hot," laughed Marcus, mopping his brow. "Isn't that breeze good?"

"Yes, yes," breathed Lavinia, lifting her face.

She could never get used to the wonder of the open air, the fragrance of flowers and the far fragrance of the sea, the deep life in all that flowing into her, the space about her. And now the wind came in great gusts of blessed coolness.

"Yes, yes," she repeated. "Oh, Marcus, aren't you happy?"

"Of course. Why, yes, I believe I am," spoke Marcus, marveling a little how he was forgetting Rome.

Just then there was a sudden flash of light, a deafening crack right in the air beside them. Both ponies snorted, tossed their heads, trembled for an instant and then started at a dead run. In the earlier gallop Lavinia had felt that Triga would still obey her. But now in this moment she sensed that Triga was crazy. Triga didn't know where nor how she was running. She was like an arrow let loose from a strong bow which must speed and speed until the power died out of it. Lavinia could hear the hoofs of Marcus' Ventus pounding behind her. But Ventus was a little smaller, and Triga, now that she was fairly started, was swifter. Meanwhile Lavinia was sticking on. She clamped her knees against the pony's sides and, unhorsemanlike, clasped her arms around the neck. She was frightened. Triga was running away. Yes, it could be that perhaps in a few moments she herself would be killed. But underneath the fright was a strange stillness in which she enjoyed this experience. She no longer felt the galloping rhythm—this was only a beating pulse of speed, speed and a gale whistling past. "She'll go ahead on the straight road," said Lavinia's queer still reasoning, "and as long as she does, I can hang on."

The rain was pouring now in torrents. They passed a *raeda* that hastily pulled to the side of the road. As it did so the curtain broke loose and flapped in the air. Triga saw it. She wheeled, leaped the foot pavement and was out on the mountainside. Lavinia's hold on the neck kept her on. Now, like a goat, Triga went leaping over the rough ground. Indeed, it was a goat path that gave her a narrow place to go. The pine growth was thick. Triga's hoofs scarcely heard. The low juniper thickets were cushionlike on either side. "A cushion is a cushion," said Lavinia's strange inner admonisher. "Best take it even if it is only a pine bush."

She loosened her knees, threw one leg over, slid down full length, and *bump!* She was in the scratchy juniper branches. Had the ground risen up to hit her? It seemed so. Here on the mountain the storm was so present, so near that Lavinia hadn't time even to think whether she was hurt. Crash after crash of thunder, rain beating, and wind howling. Triga! Where was she? She was lost. Trogus, no one, could ever catch her. Look, look!

Lavinia jumped to her feet only to see her precious Triga bounding up the slope like a winged thing. Where her hoofs found foothold was a miracle. Only a wild-born pony could have done it, or a wild-born goat. Now her four hoofs were all together in one spot, now they spread, and she bounced into the air like a ball. It didn't seem as though she were progressing fast, yet she rapidly grew smaller. At any moment she would round a cliff and be lost to view.

Lavinia burst into tears.

"Triga, Triga, come back!" she cried out just as if Triga could understand.

How terrible it was to be up here alone in this wild place, where the spirits of the wilderness raged unchecked. Jupiter Tonans, himself, was trampling above her head and no house roof to protect her from him.

Just at this moment came a terrific blinding flash, no thunder at all. Lavinia was thrown to the ground. Yet somehow in that instant she saw Triga on the height, stand right up erect and gesture with her forefeet like a man commanding an army, then wheel completely around. Down the slopes she came hurtling, blind now with terror. She passed so close that Lavinia could hear her labored breath and snorting.

Down, down, downward! The trees hid her from view.

Lavinia got to her feet feeling queer and tingly and wondering whether she were dead. No, she wasn't dead. But she was lost.

She wanted to go down the mountain but there seemed no way down, only a confusion of heights and hollows, and all covered with low growth which a man could hardly push through. There above were the cliffs towering and the clouds rolling about them so near, so active. The Via Aurelia— that great Way which had spread itself out before them so obligingly day after day was nowhere to be seen. And for the life of her, she could not tell in which direction it lay. The nearest cliff stood with a sharp edge against the sky. Lavinia had a notion that if she could round that she would certainly see the Via Aurelia and then might somehow make her way toward it. In the heavy rain she started. She must go down into a ravine and up again. The branches scratched her hands and face and caught her hair. The sharp stones cut her feet right through the sandals. She reached the bottom of the ravine, waded the narrow torrent which had formed there, began the difficult ladderlike climb. The farther she went, the more confident she was that she would see the highroad from the cliff. The rain lessened—stopped—but she did not notice the change. Up and up she scrambled. At last she rounded the cliff. Terror of Pan! Beyond were the same heaped heights and hollows. Suddenly the sun burst through. The sun in the west as she knew—the farther side of the road, and it was behind her. All this while she had labored and worked straight *away* from the Via Aurelia.

Instead of being thankful that she now at least knew her direction, the Panic terror utterly confused her. She dropped down in a heap, sobbing and shaking almost as she had when she thought she must marry Decimus. How long she crouched there she never knew, but gradually she heard what she thought was the far-away note of a bird. Repeated—repeated. Now it was louder. Oh, it was voices, real voices calling, "Aioo—Aioo—" Then, "Lavinia—Lavinia."

The joy, the change was so great that she jumped to her feet, weightless and strong.

"Aioo—Aioo," she called back. "I am here—here—"

She pushed to the edge of the cliff. She had nothing to wave except her arms, but these she waved frantically. Now far below, shoulder-deep in the underbrush, she saw Trogus. His face looked up. He must have seen her. Yes, for at that moment she saw another figure dart ahead of Trogus—pushing the undergrowth, struggling up toward her.

It was Marcus. She started toward him.

"Stay where you are," came the faint clear sound of his voice. "I'm coming."

Then he was there close.

He seized both her shoulders and shook her roughly.

"Are you killed? Are you hurt? Sister! Sister!"

"No, I'm all right," she tried to tell him in shaken laughter.

"But your face! And look at that gash on your arm. Triga threw you!" He shook her more roughly than ever. "Oh, I couldn't stand it, I tell you. I thought you were up here broken to pieces, bleeding like those wretches in the arena. I thought I'd never see you again. I thought—"

Suddenly Marcus burst into tears and sobbed unashamedly.

"Why, Marcus," said the amazed Lavinia, "I'm all right. What is the matter?"

"Triga came back without you. We were forever finding you."

"Don't be so worried," said Lavinia sensibly. "Father won't scold you. It was all my fault."

"Father? What do you mean? Father?"

Marcus stopped sobbing and looked at her wrathfully.

"Why, I thought Father," faltered Lavinia, "maybe he'd be angry."

"By Pollux, do you think I'm that kind of coward? Afraid of my father? You were up here by yourself, I tell you. These savage Ligurians could have carried you off. Anything might have happened—anything. I was sure I'd never see you again."

He looked at her fixedly for a moment, as if to make sure she was there.

Suddenly it dawned upon Lavinia that Marcus loved her. That to Marcus it meant much to have his sister alive and near. She was so astonished that tears welled right over her eyes and began to roll down her cheeks.

"Now look here," said Marcus, "don't you get sentimental and weak. We've got a Hades of a climb over these mountains before we get back to the road."

Trogus had been standing there breathless from the climb.

"Yes, little mistress—I'll help you get down," he said.

So the three started. It was a terrific scramble. Lavinia constantly marveled how she had got through by herself. But in spite of it her mind quickly reverted to her pony.

"Oh, tell me, was Triga hurt? Did you catch her?"

"Yes, little mistress," answered Trogus, "we caught her on the road. She had some ugly gashes on her sides but no legs broken."

"And you'll never ride her again. That's certain," put in Marcus.

"Oh, Marcus, please, please don't say so. Please don't take my Triga away."

Again Marcus looked at her with fixed wonder.

"Well, you *are* a funny girl. Don't you hate her for what she did? I'd like to kill her."

"Oh no, no, please, Marcus. It's natural for ponies to run away. I'll talk to her and tell her about it. She'll understand."

"Now you're just crazy," said Marcus. "Understand—a pony. Do you mean to say you'd ever be willing to get on her back again?"

"I'd like to, right away quick, before she forgets. I'll talk to her and drive her slowly and comfort her."

"I told you," interrupted Trogus, "that young mistress is a natural rider."

They found their party of travelers in great confusion. The mules had stampeded and spilled their packs. The curtains of Aurelia's *raeda* were torn. The slaves were still frightened out of their wits at the storm. And even the soldiers had set to praying loudly to Jupiter and Mithra. Aurelia, like many timid women, was the strength of everything in a crisis. She was quieting the slaves, directing them how to repack the mules, rescuing the broken objects.

She had not heard of Lavinia's mishap until most of the time of it had elapsed. And now she met her return with joyous welcome.

As for Favonius, he was intensely busy getting the whole procession in order again and planning for the night.

Chapter Nine

AFTER GENUA, the way of the Roman wanderers led, strangely enough, southwest and often straight south. For here the Sinus Lugusticus or Ligurian Gulf cuts so deeply into the land as to take full possession of the shore and control its own directions. Here the mountains no longer held aloof, soaring into the inland sky, but they crowded down, dominant to the shore. Here the sea met them with angry protest. White breakers that leaped high up the cliffs and tore them, too, with their power. But at other times, as in this April season, the sea met the mountains in quiet. The whole sea was an azure acquiescence as far as the travelers could see. The union of those two beauties, mountain and ocean, created a vast peace that made Lavinia almost breathless as hour after hour she gazed upon it. For centuries had this shore been loved by men. The Phoenicians had sought it; the Greeks had planted cities here; and in every case the fierce Ligurians and Gauls had fought them back. For they too loved this enchanted Riviera. Now the Romans had full possession, and the towns which the travelers came to were as completely Roman as those of Latium and Eturia.

They passed Savo, Albiganum, Lucus Bormani, Monoecus—Latin names all. At Monoecus the road ran up over the mountain turn after turn, height after height, and Aurelia made Lavinia abandon her half-wild pony and come into the steady *raeda*. The curtains were left open. Somehow it seemed too dangerous to be closed up when the *raeda* was edging along such terrific cliffs as if on the cornice of some gigantic roof.

"Look, Mother," said Lavinia, gazing down, down, down, upon the sea. "The ocean seems floating above itself in the air."

"But it isn't," said the literal Aurelia. "It's only because we are so high up."

"But watch it, Mother, watch the ships; they seem to be in the air too."

"Sure enough they do," assented Aurelia.

For the sea from that loftiness had a curious lifted quality, as though the water was not resting on anything but floating in space. The ship's sail and galleys also seemed suspended as Lavinia's keener eyes had noted. The galleys looked like tiny birds with wings outspread. Their banks of oars beat down upon the sea, sparkling white and silver foam. But again "They are not on the sea," cried Lavinia delightedly. "They are in the air."

Nor was this Tyrraniun sea just blue. It was the blue of fire burning clear and steady—a blue light that seemed to glow up through it from beneath. Lavinia felt as if some enchantment were overcoming her.

At night the Claudian party seldom stayed at a villa. The villa owners were unknown to them here. As for the inns, they were impossible, and in this fine weather it was no hardship to sleep in the *raedas* or even in the open. Night after night they would draw up in some little grove of pines and there Lavinia would sleep beside her mother. Father and Marcus would be almost within touch. Lavinia, too happy to sleep, would look out at the stars, smell the fragrance of pines, breathe the freshness of the sea. Once when the *raeda* was closed she heard stealthy footsteps cracking the twigs and, peeping out, she saw a fat little bear. He suspected human beings and was sitting up on his haunches like a tiny brown man, lifting his nose in the moonlight. Sniffing, sniffing, so funny, so appealing. Then as Lavinia stirred the curtains down he went on all fours and made off in a panic.

Yes, it was enchantment. Yet Lavinia knew she herself was real. She knew it especially at meal times. Dindia, their head cook-slave, was with them, and all the scullery maids. These prepared the meals which were eaten in the open. Sometimes procuring the food was a pretty adventure. Lettuce was sold to them from farm gardens, apples from the caves where the farmers had stored them, cabbage, which all Romans loved, ducks also and dressed fowl. Of course they had brought along plenty of wheat grain. Dindia would set the maids pounding it in mortars in the twilight. Then the porridge next morning would be the best ever eaten. Indeed, Lavinia longed for mealtime, would feel so empty and hungry waiting that she could hardly stand it. She had never been like this in Rome. Meals were a bore. Mother had to have all sorts of dainties made for her to persuade her to eat, and half the time Lavinia would leave them untasted. She had been an exquisite patrician maiden who must be humored. No such thing now.

One day the soldiers procured from a mountain shepherd a goat which they killed and dressed. Then at every halt they made a stew over a camp fire. All soldiers could cook. The smell of the stew came on the evening air to the *raedas*.

"Sister," said Marcus, "let's go back and see the soldiers eat."

So together they went along the high-ridged footpath by the roadside. Presently they came to the flickery light of the soldiers' camp fire. The great kettle hanging over it, in soldier fashion—gypsy fashion—eternal human fashion. One soldier had just dipped out his mess into his helmet and was sitting by the roadside, the helmet between his knees, fishing out the gobbets of meat with his fingers, chewing with his white teeth, sipping the gravy with loud sibilants.

Marcus wrinkled up his nose in the way he used to do in babyhood. Then he laughed.

"Don't you wish you could dip in too?" he asked Lavinia.

"No, I wouldn't eat goat," said Lavinia properly.

"What a falsehood!" quoth Marcus.

Lavinia laughed with him.

"Yes, that was a lie. I want that meat and that gravy and the turnips and cabbage and onions—everything. And I don't care a bit about its being goat."

The man, a desert Arab, looked up at them. He could not understand Latin but he could understand human hunger. He reached out the helmet to them.

Marcus took a bit of the dripping meat and thanked him. Then Lavinia did also.

"Let's go back quick," she told Marcus. "Let's go back to our own supper before we do anything more disgraceful."

But it was two very sturdy young Romans that went running back along the Via Aurelia to their own more proper camp.

The weather was perfect—the famous Riviera weather, in

the famous Riviera season. Day after day Phoebus rose over the mountains, stepped across the wide pathway of the sky, unhampered by any cloud. Every evening he dipped into the sea with unspeakable glory.

The travelers left behind the crag of Monoecus. The road came down shoreward. They passed the ancient Greek city of Nicaea neglected by the Romans, who had built their own prosperous town of Cemendlum up in the hills. They did not stop at either place, for Favonius was growing impatient to reach his destination, and the weather favored him.

But even the most trusted climate can play tricks, lose its temper in the midst of the most mellifluous season. A cold damp wind blew down from the snow-capped Alps, met the warm sea, and created thick fog. Thunder and lightning hurtled through the fog blanket and a gusty rain set in. It was unseasonable, unexpected, abominable! But there it was. The travelers searched out their heaviest cloaks from the baggage, crouched behind the curtains of *raeda* or of freight wagon, or plodded along head forward on foot against the wind. The road was mountainous again. Night had fallen moonless and impenetrable. They were afraid of being run down by vehicles in the dark.

All of a sudden lights showed through the mist. The cavalcade drew up in front of the dimly lighted doorway.

"Wait here," Favonius told Aurelia, "while I go in and see what we have found."

Lavinia peered out of the curtains, wondering what adventure came now. She was tired and cold, could hardly wait for her father's delay.

At last he came and stood by the *raeda* in the rain.

"It's one of the government *mansiones*," he told Aurelia. "And surly fellows they are in charge. But we'll have to stay here. They keep telling me it is only five miles to Forum Julii, but the last milestone read fifteen, so they're plainly lying."

"Heaven help us," breathed Aurelia.

"And all the gods besides," laughed Favonius. "Come, hurry, Lavinia, Marcus."

They entered an archway lofty enough for the carts and *raedas* and found themselves in an oblong courtyard. It was dirty and had an ancient complicated smell from which a clean Roman shrank as from a blow. Lavinia could see the hindquarters and tails of donkeys and horses whose stalls lined the court. The whole lower floor was for animals and slaves.

"What rooms have you?" Favonius was asking of the host, a stocky mountaineer who stood bowing.

"We can give you maybe two rooms," said the man. "But, master"—he hesitated—"the Emperor's messenger is expected tonight. We have to keep rooms for him and his men and places for his horses."

"Two rooms will do," said Favonius.

"Master—the soldiers—must we receive them?"

"No," said Favonius shortly. "They've found some caves near by up the road and prefer to stay in them. (Don't blame 'em)," Favonius added under his breath.

"Oh, thank ye—thank ye—master." The man bowed to the ground, then snapped erect, looking as if he had not bowed at all. He led the way up a rickety stair that led to a gallery which surrounded the whole court. Upon this gallery opened the second-story rooms. He showed Favonius and Aurelia to one near at hand, then started toward the back of the quadrangle for the rooms for Lavinia and Marcus.

"Never mind—never mind," Favonius said with command. "You say you're to be crowded. Give us one room—one room only, with four couches."

Aurelia looked her amazement but said nothing.

"Master," ventured the man, "that isn't necessary. We can give ye two rooms."

"One room with four couches," repeated Favonius Claudius—in a voice that made the man jump.

They entered the close room, clammy like a tomb. After some confusion the couches were brought. Durus, Favonius' special body slave, with some others was bringing up great armfuls of blankets from the Roman carts. As soon as the inn servants had departed, Favonius spoke in a low tone to Aurelia.

"There's probably no danger, but I don't like the looks of this place nor the ways of the men. We four"—he turned to Marcus and Lavinia—"will sleep in this one place. Durus, you also will sleep on the floor. And you"—turning to the four other slaves—"sleep outside on the balcony. Durus, go down to your mistress's *raeda* and get out four swords which are hidden there."

Favonius himself and Marcus were, of course, armed. And both wore leather corselets that would turn a sword thrust.

"Favonius," whispered Aurelia, "are we in such danger? Why do we stay? The place is horrible, horrible."

"I'm over-careful," said Favonius. "The place is a government *mansio*. The sign of the Emperor's Postal Service is over the gateway. The number of horse stalls, the place for storage—all show it."

"Then what is the matter?"

Favonius Claudius gave a short laugh. "Just a foolish admonition of the gods. Something about the place, something in the air. It doesn't concern us—for we are strangers. But we'd best be ready."

Durus entered, armed and wrapped in his cloak. Lavinia

and Marcus wrapped themselves each in a blanket and lay down on their couches. Aurelia and Favonius did likewise, and Durus lay on the floor. It is doubtful if anyone slept. It seemed incredible that after their carefree days of sunshine they should suddenly find themselves so situated.

Lavinia's couch seemed to be composed of bricks. Such humps and hollows. Nor was it free of small living enemies, whose attentions kept her jumping. But she was healthy and tired, and at last fell asleep.

She was roused by a terrible piercing cry. She seemed coming up from a great depth of slumber and realized that this was not the first cry she heard. Her father was already dressed and at the curtained doorway. Aurelia was shivering on her feet. Marcus was just behind his father.

"Marcus, stay here," pleaded Aurelia.

"No, I need him," answered Favonius. "He must come."

"Come, Durus."

They threw open the curtain and stepped out on the balcony. As they did so there came from the confused noise below a hideous gulping sound. Lavinia had never heard such a sound in her life. But she instinctively knew that the man who made it was in the act of death—and that from a sudden blow. She screamed with terror. Her heart pounded like a hammer. And now the noise increased—the grind of sword striking shield, the blows of cudgels, yells—groans of effort, groans of pain. It was like nothing so much as a large, close-gripped dog fight. So wolves might sound in the pack fighting over their kill.

Lavinia ran to the open curtain and looked out. A smoky torch showed dimly the scene. Men close-locked like wolves indeed—a writhing mass. The frightened horses broken loose from their stalls rearing fearfully in the crowd. At the front archway were men in armor on horses. She was just in time to see her father and Marcus leap over the balcony onto the shoulders of the fighters and Durus, that gigantic man, leap after them. Sorry the man on whom Durus fell!

"Lavinia, come here at once," cried Aurelia. And Lavinia was only too glad to obey. She clung to her mother while the slaves outside stood ready to defend the bedroom doorway. Suddenly Clotho, Aurelia's maid, came running from her room below.

"Oh, mistress! It's some Roman soldiers trying to get in, and the men of the inn fightin' 'em. Oh, mistress! ye never saw the like. There was men sprang from every horse stall—every corner—hundreds and hundreds—hiding, hiding everywhere, and all of 'em with clubs and swords an' makin' at the Romans."

She fell on her knees and clung to Aurelia's knees.

"Oh, mistress, how'd I ever get through them? How'd I ever get through the crowd?"

"Be still," spoke Aurelia. "You're here now. Don't be afraid."

"Oh, mistress, why did Master jump down?"

"I don't know, Clotho. But Master knows best. Lavinia, stop crying."

And Lavinia suddenly realized that she was sobbing bitterly and had been ever since she had heard the man die in the courtyard. She tried to quiet herself, clinging to her mother and feeling like a very miserable little girl, instead of a young lady of thirteen.

Now they were aware of a great shout. Some Gallic signal they did not understand, and the noise trailed off, diminishing, diminishing, running footsteps at the back of the inn, at the front, too, galloping hoofs on the hard road. Then silence—terrible silence.

Even Aurelia had to go to the door now. And Lavinia tightly held her mother's hand. They looked over. The torch still smoked in its corner like a faithful sentinel. But the place was deserted—that is, deserted save for the dead lying on the earthen floor, and the moving figures of Favonius and Durus. Or was it Favonius?

"Favonius, Favonius Claudius!" called Aurelia, clear and ringing.

"Yes, dear, I'm here," came Favonius' voice. Oh, blessed sound! All safe now.

"Where, where is Marcus?"

"He's here too. Just a little scratch. We'll be up in a moment."

Hardly breathing, they waited.

Here came Favonius up the stair and Durus—helping Marcus between them. Aurelia ran to them, not even daring to ask.

"A broken ankle," Favonius informed them, "and a wound in the arm. He should have defended himself better."

"I'm all right—all right," said Marcus, then groaned as his ankle shot some pain. "They were so crowded, Father. I couldn't look all ways at once."

"Well, that's the duty of a soldier. But it was your first fight."

"Master, he fought off three, nay four. You didn't see him."

Favonius laughed. He was pleased with Marcus. Just not showing it.

"Ah, Durus, you were always soft on your young master," Favonius Claudius reproved him. But he fooled nobody, Marcus least of all.

They sat Marcus on a couch, held his arm high, and tried to staunch his wound.

"I wish we had some hot water," said Aurelia.

"Well, we haven't, dear. We'll have to do our best."

"I saw the well," Clotho whispered to Aurelia. "It's in the left corner of the court."

"Mistress, I'll get ye some water an' soon too," said Durus in a low tone.

He went hurrying off—ordering the slaves to help him. Claudius' party seemed to be in full possession. No one there but their own party. Even the horses and mules were gone—the supplies of fodder and food gone too. The Gallic innkeepers had made off with the whole supply of the post, and were now in their mountain fastness. The soldiers of Claudius' party, hearing the fracas, had come running from the caves. A short while and they and Durus had dragged the dead to shelter, found the kitchen supply of wood, lighted a great fire in the open court.

"That will burn out some of their cursed smell," said Durus—who, though no Roman himself, had learned to love Roman cleanliness.

He found Dindia's clean kettles and soon one of them was boiling over the fire. Durus brought the hot water, and Lavinia bathed Marcus' ankle while Aurelia bathed and wrapped his arm. Lavinia threw her arms about Marcus and kissed him—but he pushed her off with great manliness.

"Pooh—it's nothing. Why such a fuss?"

They were so busy that they did not notice the slow light of dawn nor that the rain had stopped. The slaves cleaned a space about the fire and brought the couches and blankets. Here sat Favonius and his family, and here Marcus tried to rest. Here they ate an early breakfast, eager to be gone from the ill-smelling, fateful place.

"But what was it, Favonius? What was the fight about?" asked Aurelia. "Do you know?"

"Yes, I know well. These *mansiones* are hated by the provincials who are obliged to care for them. Hated like the gates of Hades. They have been always, even since the Republic. The *mansiones* now belong to the Emperor, and all along the roads they are the stations for the Emperor's legates and messengers. The local people have to build them, furnish the horses and mules and fodder and food and room for the messengers when they arrive. Furnish all, indeed, whatever the messengers demand. So they hate the messengers with great hatred. Gods, how they yelled at that fellow by the gate. Poor fellow, he's paid for it with his life."

One of the slaves sitting on the ground stirred uneasily.

"Well, sirrah," said Favonius, "what is it you know? What is it you want to tell?"

The man scrambled to his feet.

"I'm not sayin' they did right, master—these Gallic slaves."

"Right, right! That's none of your business to say nor think about. What do you know?"

The man trembled where he stood. "I heard 'em in one of the horse stalls. They didn't know I was next the partition. This man—the messenger of the Emperor—had cuffed 'em about when he was here a week ago on his way to Nemausis. He was carryin' a message from the Emperor. They was afraid of him." The man stopped.

"Well—well," Favonius encouraged him.

"When he went off he stole the innkeeper's daughter. They was mad."

"Did you hear them planning the fight?"

"No, master."

"Master," spoke up another slave, "there was men in every horse stall. Men in a crowd outside waitin' as still as still. An' they had pack mules all packed."

"You should have reported that."

"They caught me lookin', master. They said they'd kill me."

Favonius kept a scowling silence. Then he asked,

"How did they know the messenger would come tonight?"

"I don't know, master. But they expected him from Nemausis."

"Well, he's dead now," said Favonius Claudius sadly, "and two of his companions. A big price to pay for a miserable peasant girl."

All Favonius' sympathy was for the young Romans. But Lavinia kept thinking of the poor frightened girl torn from her home. Nobody seemed to know where she was, nor to care. What would she herself do if she were stolen like that?

"Well—we must be going," ordered Favonius briskly. "I'll have to report this at Forum Julii—a horrid business."

Chapter Ten

OWING to their early start, the travelers reached Forum Julii by midmorning. Here Favonius Claudius made his report of rebellion and murder in the *mansio* and thus occasioned no little excitement among the Julians. They went pouring down the road in crowds, whether in regret or rejoicing for the native victory it would be hard to say. After all, none of them was of Roman blood though many had Roman citizenship.

Forum Julii proved to be an important town. It had been founded almost a hundred years before by Julius Caesar when he gave land to his veterans. This was a common way of rewarding Roman soldiers when their term of service was over. Forum Julii had its circus, still unfinished but designed to seat nine thousand spectators. It had great stone ramparts and, as its name implied, a fine Forum. Lavinia searched out her father's traveling cup and found the town's name thereon, marveling how far along the list it stood.

"See, Mother, how far we have come," she announced proudly, tracing the names with her finger.

"Oh, daughter, daughter, put it away," sighed Aurelia.

"They are all distances from Rome. And now we are distant indeed."

What would have been their wonder could they have known that some day this handsome Forum Julii would shrink to a mere village within its wide-stretched walls? And that its sonorous name on barbarian lips would wear down to the short word Frejus.

The hardships of the night told on Aurelia. But Favonius and Marcus were the heroes of the hour. A prominent citizen of the town insisted on their coming to his seaside villa for at least the night. Here his wife met them with great respect and showed Aurelia every attention. They were Iberians and spoke a strange jargon of Latin, but their villa was true Roman, clean, spacious, set on a height with splendid views of the sea and, to Favonius' delight, a complete Roman bath. What a comfort it was to wash away all traces of the inn's filth, to have tunics, togas and blankets washed by the slaves of their kind hosts, even the horses curried and well fed. Marcus was put in a cool spacious room on a terrace. Here his ankle was wrapped in hot compresses while Aurelia directed the treatment. Then Lavinia stayed with him all the day through. Sometimes she wandered out to the colonnades and lovely gardens, but only to hurry back to tell Marcus everything she saw.

"I want to see it too," complained Marcus.

"Well, it isn't so pretty as it ought to be because the wind blows so hard. It is cutting the new flowers to pieces."

Marcus kicked viciously with his good leg.

"Anyway, I want to go out to see. I don't like it in here."

However, the hot-water treatment reduced his ankle, and Favonius, feeling it expertly, found it was not broken, only badly bruised and cut by a sword.

"You'll soon be walking about, son," he pronounced. "By Jupiter Ammon—if it had been really broken, it would never be really strong and trustworthy for soldiering."

They stayed for two days and so found themselves completely refreshed. With many thanks to their host they took their departure. Even Marcus was comfortable for travel, lying on the cushions of his *raeda*.

But trouble never comes singly. The rains had washed out the direct road to Arlate so the travelers had to go around north by way of Segustera. This road strikes inland among the jagged mountains later to be called the mountains of the Moors because of the wild bandits there—later yet l'Estrel. Wild now they are, and wilder yet they were as these Roman travelers mounted the Roman road. There were steep climbs when the horses panted and the foot travelers fell behind. The road crossed and recrossed the torrent of Druentia River.

Rocks to the Romans spelled nothing of the past world history; they were merely stone for road building, stone for palace building, marble for statue carving and the like. But these rocks of the Estrel, sometimes gray granite, sometimes grotesque volcanic forms, greatly amused Marcus and Lavinia.

"By Pollux, sister, look at that one," Marcus would call, pointing to a high pinnacle like a huge sharp spear. "Mars himself might fight with that."

Lavinia scrambled out of her *raeda* and perched herself on the edge of Marcus' litter.

"Yes, and look at that one across the ravine, like a tall man in a hood, and that one like an eagle's head. They are funny!"

And the two laughed together as the *raeda* moved onward.

Smoothly, in spite of the jagged hills, went the Roman road over secure arched bridges and causeways, leading the way for the Roman legions into the heart of the great north. For now Italia was left behind. They were in the province of Gallia. The wind still blew, cutting their faces, whirling the gravel of the wayside, and tossing cloaks into billows.

Well known was this wind, dreaded by the inhabitants of Gallia, dreaded by every successive race, and called the Mistral. The eternal snows of the Alps gave it their cruel iciness and the valley of the Rhodanus River was its free path to sweep to the Mediterranean.

Lavinia could hardly believe that the people of these mountains were human. To be sure, they walked erect instead of on all fours, but they were as shaggy as their own goats, dark, taller than Romans, clad in trousers which to Lavinia and Marcus were so ridiculous that they laughed every time they caught sight of a shepherd leaping along the heights. Their upper garment was a bright striped vest and indeed the trousers were gorgeous too. These people lived in caves and rudest stone huts which also were like lairs rather than homes. Men and women would stand on the cliffs to watch the Romans pass. Or if the party made a halt, they would steal timidly down, come near, offering pottery or flowers as gifts. The wind and the Romans' discomfort in it vastly amused them. They themselves endured it without winking. They seemed to think it blew for their benefit to afford entertainment and to let them laugh at the Romans' discomfort.

Arlate was reached the seventh day. To Lavinia's amazement they entered a splendid city. She had never heard of Arlate, nor had Marcus. Favonius, of course, had known its name as a colony of Rome. They passed the Arlatan tombs by the roadside—fine marble tombs—they came to an august gate in the city walls, and then proceeded through many streets to the Forum where colonnades of marble and marble statues surrounded the whole. They had not even begun to inquire their way when a well-dressed slave met them.

"The duovirus expects you," he said in good Latin. "May I lead you to his home?"

"But why should I go to his home?" inquired Favonius.

"Are you not Favonius Claudius, Roman patrician, traveling to Britannia at the Emperor's request?"

"Yes."

"Word came from Forum Julii that you were coming hither and my master, Agathocles, wishes to entertain you."

Thus did news travel on the Roman roads apparently on wings.

Here Agathocles himself came hurrying up. He would not take no for answer; Clio, his wife, was expecting them; all was ready. So it was that the travelers found themselves again in a comfortable home, not a villa but a town house on a height above the river. This home, though not so rich, was more beautiful than the villa at Forum Julii. The atrium was pure Greek and Doric. The statues were Greek; even the altar was for Apollo rather than Vesta. Agathocles was himself Greek, a judge of the city, dignified, kindly, merry. Favonius had to like him, and Aurelia soon felt at ease with the lovely Clio.

As for Lavinia and Marcus, they were entertained by two young girls their own age, Neraea and Delphinia. Great was the sorrow over Marcus' misfortune. But they had known of it beforehand, and their mother had provided a special room for him. Yes, they knew of the treatment and the hot water was ready—the slaves only waited.

They left Marcus beautifully established and the girls led Lavinia to her room.

"We hope you'll like it," said the eldest. "It's Neraea's room and from the little atrium there's a view of the river."

"But why should Neraea give me her room?" spoke Lavinia timidly. "I can sleep anywhere just so it's near Mother."

"It's near your mother; see, her room is across the atrium yonder."

But Lavinia was still timid, still ill at ease. "What will they think of me?" her heart was asking of her heart. "They are so beautiful—oh yes, both of them—one couldn't choose."

Their faces were like pure ivory, their black hair that waved so sweetly from the middle parting and swept over their ears to the pretty knot nestling at the neck. They wore strange Gallic pins in their hair, gold filigree with flecks of turquoise. What lovely eyes! Oh! what lovely, lovely eyes! Suppose they knew that Decimus had run away to Spain rather than marry Lavinia. Suppose they knew he had called her ugly. Right in the Roman Forum. They'd laugh. They would be laughing right now.

But Delphinia and Neraea were not laughing; they were showing her an enameled comb and mirror she was to use.

"And the bath is ready," Delphinia was saying kindly. "You can go in now with your lady mother."

"Yes—yes," spoke Lavinia's low voice, "I'll go to the bath."

Afterward she dreaded to meet the girls. By this time they would have talked her over. Her tunic and toga worn and faded from the trip. Her hair roughened with the wind. She had not tidied up to enter the town. There seemed nothing in her baggage that was fit to wear.

She found the girls waiting near her room.

"You look so rested from the bath," said Delphinia with encouragement.

"Yes—yes, I do feel better."

"Do you suppose your brother feels better too?" spoke up Neraea.

"He's really all right," answered Lavinia. "He just isn't used to staying still."

"Do you suppose he is bored?"

At this Lavinia had to laugh.

"Bored! You should see him. He kicks with his feet and says 'by Pollux' and 'by Jupiter.' I have to stay with him all the time."

Neraea clapped her hands together as if somehow she had attained an object. Her lovely eyes shone star-like.

"Let's go and entertain him—all of us. You take us to his room."

Lavinia was astonished. No Roman girl would do so. No Roman girls she knew. Yet it was all kind, childlike almost.

"Wait," said Neraea. "We can't entertain him just by going in and staring at him and saying how's your foot, poor dear. I'll get my lyre and, Delphinia, have Tychichus bring your organ."

"Wait for us here." She turned to Lavinia. "See, now I don't even know your name."

Lavinia told her and in a kind of daze watched them run across the atrium for their musical instruments. Now they returned. Two slaves were carrying a thing Lavinia had never seen—like a huge Pandaean pipe—the pipes gilded, and a row of flats below—perhaps to play upon.

Another slave carried the familiar lyre. Both girls were laughing as if upon some great lark.

"You go in first, Lavinia," they said. "We don't dare. See, it's that way, the next atrium—do you remember?"

Lavinia pushed back the curtain and found Marcus lying flat on his couch in the dim room. His arms were flung above his head, his face scowling.

"You've been away forever, Lavinia," he began crossly. "Why didn't you come?"

"Hist—hist, Marcus. The young ladies are with me."

But the young ladies were already in the room. They made a graceful bow together.

"We heard," said Neraea, "that a certain young gentleman was wounded while defending the Emperor's messenger. We have come to make him forget his wounds and his pain."

Forget! Marcus looked as if he had forgotten his whole past life and could only remember that two nymphs had appeared by magic at his bedside. Lavinia had to laugh at his utter surprise, embarrassment.

"But—but I didn't know you were coming. I'd have put on my other tunic. I'd have"—suddenly Marcus was himself again—"put on a crown of laurel and poured out the sacrificial cup of wine."

"No sacrifice is necessary, save music which we are providing. Oh—but it's dark and close in here; wouldn't you rather be out in the sunny corridor?"

"I surely would," declared Marcus. "Then perhaps I can believe that you are real."

They laughed at this—not loudly, but unconscious happy laughter as pretty as the music they were about to make. The slaves put down the organ and carried Marcus on his couch out into the sunny space where there were green vines and flowers. Then the slaves set the organ on its pillar, adjusted it with its tank of water and bellows, and began to pump. Delphinia's white, skillful fingers ran over the keys and Neraea stood ready to sing.

But alas, the sounds that came forth were terrible hoots and squeals, then the air would exhaust and the organ would give a dying gurgle. Tychichus pumped as though he were chopping wood, and that made it worse.

Lavinia pressed her hands tight together. Poor Delphinia, poor girl, she had come in so proudly to play for the stranger and now this disgraceful fiasco. Delphinia bent low over the keys. Her shoulders were shaking.

Suddenly she sprang to her feet. She was in gales of laughter. She turned to the organ, gesturing toward it with her musician hands.

"You disgraceful thing," she called it, "showing off like a dog fight before the young Roman. And I thought you were such a wonderful new invention. Shame on you. Take it away, Tychichus, and bring my lute."

Marcus laughed; Neraea laughed. Before Lavinia realized she was laughing, too, and the atrium rang with that sweetest of all sounds, the boundless joy of youth.

"She might have scolded the slave," thought Lavinia. "For it was he who made a mess of it."

But even the slave did not seem to expect a scolding. He soon returned with the lute, placed it in Delphinia's hands, and put the lute ribbon around her neck. Neraea sat down with the lyre on her knee. Then began the sweetest birdlike tinkle of pure old music, and the two voices joined lifted in a melody that went round and round like bees in a circle always returning to the refrain which called the various birds to come back to the north because spring was come. First Delphinia would sing the refrain, then Neraea, and each time it was in a new and higher key, so that the little song itself seemed lifting and flying.

Marcus sat up, his eyes round as a baby's, listening.

"Another," he begged when they finished, "please, another."

Then they sang a song of Arlate, the beautiful city by the

river, telling how no one ever wanted to leave Arlate, and how all longed to return no matter how long away.

"I'll surely want to return," declared Marcus.

Then they sang a sad song inquiring, "Where are the roses of yesteryear?"

Then Neraea by herself sang a song about the nightingale.

There seemed no end of the songs they knew, these two Arlatiennes. They sang until a slave came to call them to the cena, which, country fashion, was served in the middle of day. All the family were at the dining table, the judge, his wife, the daughters and three little sons, Favonius and his family, and Marcus' couch was carried in.

Lavinia was perfectly happy. She had completely forgotten her self-conscious jealousy. Marcus forgot his bruised ankle; Aurelia talked familiarly with Clio and was happier than she had been at any time on the journey. Favonius was happy.

Chapter Eleven

AVONIUS REMAINED HAPPY until next day. Then he came to Aurelia, his face clouded with anxiety.

"A messenger has just arrived," he told her, "a special messenger to me from Pompeius Falco in Britannia. It's an order for me to remain in Arlate and await the arrival of a contingent of soldiers from Iberia. It seems I am to conduct them to Britannia."

"Well," said Aurelia, "is there any harm in that? We are certainly comfortable here and seem welcome. And it gives Marcus time to recover."

But Favonius' face clouded yet more.

"It looks unnecessary to me—this order. Very peremptory—as if Falco wanted to let me know even before I get there that I am to be at his beck and call. Why can't the soldiers go north under their present leader?"

Of course Aurelia could not answer this.

"Falco is an upstart of Hadrian's making," Favonius went on. "He knows the Emperor has no love for me so he wants to show he hasn't either."

Aurelia was troubled. Falco was the new governor of

Britain. Favonius had not met him. But he had heard no good of him. Aurelia kept steady.

"After all," she said, "the troops may have an incompetent leader. It may be more necessary than you think."

She laid her hand on Favonius' arm. She hated to have him harassed by people in authority. Favonius himself should be the one in authority, so she thought.

Favonius took her hand and held it. He was proud of Aurelia's hand. It had a patrician shape well known in Rome.

"I wouldn't worry," she went on. "Our arrival in Britannia will look more important with a troop of the legionary. And you know, Favonius, how easily you gain the loyalty of your men. By the time you get to Britannia these troops will be your very own. No matter where the governor sends them."

"Do you think so?"

"I know so, Favonius. That has always been your experience."

Now Aurelia was smiling. She quite believed what she was saying. It was this faith-courage of Aurelia's which Favonius depended on.

"You're right, of course you're right. It was the messenger's surly manner that misled me."

When the young folk heard of the prolonged visit, they were charmed.

"Are you glad, Lavinia?" asked Neraea, throwing her arms about Lavinia's waist.

"Yes, yes, I'll love to stay," she answered.

"Do you know, Lavinia, we thought at first you were proud because you came from Rome."

"Oh no! no, no—I wasn't proud," earnestly spoke Lavinia and with a sudden catch in her voice.

"But surely you didn't like us."

"Oh, I did—but I thought, I thought—"

The remembrance of Decimus came clear again and Lavinia turned her face away.

"I thought surely you couldn't like me, because—well, because you and Delphinia are so beautiful."

"Well, I've heard of the famous geese of Rome and I guess you're one of them. Little goose!"

Neraea lifted Lavinia's chin lovingly and looked into her face.

"Now how could we fail to like you, yes, right away, first sight?—how could anyone?"

"I—I don't know," Lavinia faltered, but she, too, began to laugh at her own fears.

"Let's go riding," proposed Delphinia. "Our hostler says you have a white pony. We have ponies too."

So the three ponies were brought with the escort of slaves. Trogus with Triga in charge. Marcus was indignant at their going. He came down to the courtyard hobbling on the crutches Trogus had made him and protested strongly.

"Pony riding's no sport for girls. People might think you were soldiers' or farmers' wives."

"But, Marcus," began Lavinia, "you were the one—" She stopped. Yes, Marcus was the one who had begged for the pony for her. It was entirely by his kindness that she could ride at all. Was it just for her now to go off and leave him? Justice meant much to this daughter of the Romans. She looked at Delphinia, at Neraea. . . .

"Do you mind," she pleaded, "if I stay at home with Marcus? I want to go. You will understand?"

"No, I won't understand," answered Neraea. "I want you to go and see our wonderful plains and the wild horses. For you'll never have another chance. I'll stay with Marcus."

Marcus almost dropped a crutch.

"Will you, Neraea? Oh, you're my goddess for today! Will you sing 'the Nightingale?'"

"Do goddesses sing?" laughed Neraea, patting her pony's neck.

"Well, they'd be glad to, if they could sing like you." Lavinia marveled at all these pretty speeches suddenly coming from Marcus. There was no use to argue; he and Neraea were already going off together. And no regret for the ride was apparent in either of them.

The ride was splendid. The roads were winding dirt roads leading over the flattest country Lavinia had ever seen. There were no real trees—only low scrub oaks and pine bushes and the wiry silvery grass stretched away and away to where the sky came down.

"It is like an ocean," said the delighted Lavinia. "See, when the wind blows there are waves of grass." How big the world was in this open space—striking awe to the tiny riders who went galloping in the midst of that great flat world. All the world was flat, so these girls believed, like a big flat cake—oh, flatter than a cake. The salt wind blew strongly from the sea which was only ten miles away. Not the cruel Mistral but refreshing, invigorating.

The Rhone at Arlate spreads out and separates into a delta. The miles of flat plain are the gift of the Rhone.

"Look! look!" cried Delphinia. "There they are on the edge of the lake—the horses."

Far off could be seen a huddled restless mass, about the color of the silvery salt grass. Delphinia pointed her pony's head toward them, and Lavinia followed. These herds of ponies were utterly wild and free, like wandering birds. It would be a thrilling experience to see horses that had never been broken. The girls did not notice that the two grooms moved closer, riding within touching distance. Now they could see the horses' heads, most of them pointing away from the wind and lowered grazing, their tails switching, switching at the flies. Now the girls were quite near—a splendid view.

Suddenly the leader of the herd lifted his head and neighed; Triga quivered and neighed in response; Delphinia's horse neighed like a trumpet; then both horses started at a dead run toward their free comrades.

Instantly Trogus was at Lavinia's side. He grabbed the halter, jerking and commanding Triga.

"Hold hard, little mistress. I'll turn her," he yelled. And turn her he did, though Triga reared and plunged.

"Whip her, whip her," Trogus commanded, and Lavinia laid it on well—for she knew this was a time to obey Trogus. Poor Triga trembled and pelted along, but she was used to obeying Trogus now. Lavinia had no time to see that Delphinia's hostler was doing the same for her. But she could hear him yelling. The herd of horses heard him, too, and stampeded in the other direction, leaping like deer away and away into the distance.

"And a good thing too," commented the breathless Trogus. "If they had come after us they're as fierce as bulls—regular fighters."

Delphinia was pale and shaken but recovering fast.

"There are herds of wild cattle too," she said. "But next time we won't ride toward them. That was foolish."

Next day Lavinia devoted herself to Marcus. She was reading to him.

Suddenly Marcus interrupted her, apropos of nothing.

"Sister, did you know that Agathocles is the son of a freedman?"

"No," said Lavinia, wondering. "But how did you happen to know?"

"Trogus heard it. Lavinia, do you suppose Father will mind?"

"Mind? Why should Father mind? Isn't he accepting his hospitality? Father says Agathocles is a splendid judge. He told Mother. He heard him give a decision yesterday."

"Did he? Did he?" urged Marcus, amazingly concerned. "And, Lavinia, up here in Gaul it doesn't seem to matter, being descended from freedmen. I mean—Agathocles traces his ancestry back to a noble family of Corinth. They fled from Corinth two hundred years ago, when Mummius destroyed the city. They fled to Epirus and were captured there and enslaved. But almost the whole family have bought their freedom. Agathocles' father did."

Lavinia began to read again, but again Marcus interrupted.

"Sister, did you ever think of it? It must be a dreadful thing to be made a slave when you've really noble blood and all that."

"I never thought of it," said Lavinia. "That is, not till Angelion ran away."

"I was furious at Angelion," went on Marcus. "Sister, do you suppose Trogus wishes he were free?"

Lavinia laughed. "Trogus! Never. Why, he loves all of us and the horses too. And he hasn't a care in the world. What a funny question. Trogus is part of the family."

"Yes, yes. I guess he is. Do you suppose Father knows Agathocles is the son of a freedman?"

Lavinia saw it was no use to read. Marcus wasn't fond of books anyway. There was a footstep in the sunny courtyard and Neraea was coming with her slave, carrying the lyre. Marcus had never cared for music either until he came to Arlate. But now the music seemed actually to cure him. Already he walked almost perfectly, and his grace of movement was returning.

The next morning Marcus was fully able to go with them all to the theater of Arlate to hear a play. By good luck the play was *Ion,* which Lavinia knew so well. It was to be given in Greek, for the Arlatans had not forgotten their native language, when Arlate was a Greek city before the Romans came.

It was a brilliant May morning. The marble arc of the theater shone in the light like the inside of a great pearl shell. The *scena* which backed the orchestra circle was a high wall shutting out any view beyond, and against this were slender marble columns so that it was easy to imagine that this was the temple of Delphi. Before the play began, Agathocles and Clio led them all about the theater to see the statue of Venus, the statue of Augustus, the portrait busts, the sculptures of leaves and little animals. At the Arlate Theater all the arts seemed united.

Then the play began. These plays of Euripides, acted as they were at this time, were the best the world has ever known. Favonius and Aurelia, who had studied Greek literature and philosophy, were almost pathetic in their respect for it. As for Lavinia and Marcus and their two young hostesses, they sat together, completely absorbed in the simple yet lovely music, the slow mimetic dancing of the chorus, and most of all in the swift drama which moved forward from one breathless crisis to another. Lavinia noticed that Neraea was sitting next to Marcus and in her low, clear voice translating for him all the dialogue. Marcus, who had cared only for the contests of gladiators and the fights of wild beasts, seemed to be thoroughly enjoying this milder pleasure.

Three weeks passed and then arrived the soldiery from Iberia destined for the legion in Britain. Favonius took charge of them, and early one morning in late May the travelers started again upon their journey.

Both hosts and guests were sorrowful at the parting, for they had become fast friends. Agathocles and Clio loaded them all with gifts. The cavalcade crowded the narrow Arlatan street. At the last there was a delay. Marcus was not there. Lavinia noticed that Neraea, too, was absent. Everybody waited while Trogus held Marcus' pony and Favonius looked back at the gate, angry and disturbed. At last Marcus came hurrying out, leaped on his horse at a single bound, and made off, passing the rest of the procession.

As they jogged along the river road in the *raeda*, Lavinia became more and more anxious about Marcus. At length, she asked Aurelia if she might ride with Marcus.

"Yes, dear," said Aurelia. "Indeed, I wish you would."

In a few minutes Lavinia was cantering ahead on Triga. She passed the supply wagons, her father's *raeda*, the slaves, the soldiers, and at last came upon Marcus riding steadily with his head down. She knew well what was the matter. She drove up close, laying her hand on his arm.

"I am so sorry," she said softly. "I am so, so sorry."

Marcus did not look at her.

"Father minded," he said. "He minded a lot about Agathocles' father being a slave."

"How could he?" broke out Lavinia, angry all of a sudden. "We stayed at Agathocles' house; we accepted his hospitality. And Neraea's the loveliest girl I ever knew."

This made Marcus look up.

"Do you think so?" he questioned. "Do you think so too?" Then he added, "Well, we shall never see her again."

They rode on and on in silence in the bright loveliness of the spring morning. Then Marcus spoke again.

"Sister"—he averted his face—"if you don't object, I'd rather ride alone this morning," he said.

Then Lavinia saw that the tears were coursing down Marcus' cheeks and he could not help it. With an aching heart, Lavinia turned Triga about and rode back to her mother.

Chapter Twelve

FROM ARLATE, the road ran straight northward, following the river Rhodanus, a noble river making the Arnus and the Po, which Lavinia had seen in Italia, seem but inconsiderable streams. And splendid cities stood upon its banks. The travelers passed swiftly through Tarusco and reached Avenio at nightfall. The second night was spent at Arusio. Here they entered through a triumphal arch which Augustus had built. Here they saw a theater grander than that at Arlate. Here were ramparts, forum, all that goes with a dignified Roman city.

After this the big cities were not so close together, but the sixth day of their journey brought them to Valentia. At this point the river Rhodanus flowed in a steep, wild gorge. Lavinia thought Marcus would enjoy this, but she could not make him notice anything. The tenth day brought them to Lugudunum, the finest city of all, the capital of the three Gauls. Just outside the city gates was a conspicuous marble monument attesting this fact. At Lugudunum, as at the modern Lyons, the river Rhodanus took form, by the confluence of two rivers from the north, making a magnificent waterway for traffic north and south—a waterway to be used throughout all history.

Both Favonius and Aurelia realized that here at Lugudunum was their last close contact with Rome. Lavinia and Marcus had no such regrets; they passed through the prosperous streets, taking for granted the handsome buildings, the gay bazaars, the wealthy people. But they sensed as all young people would the vitality and vigor of the place.

In fact, there was no colony in all the Roman Empire so prosperous and happy as this of Southern Gaul. No colony so fully Romanized. In Greece, Egypt, Northern Africa, Rome met with civilizations which were superior to her own. These old civilizations did not give way. Rather Rome itself conformed and was being absorbed. But here the original Celt had been simple, undeveloped. The Greeks in Gaul had been few and in scattered cities, so Roman civilization was received and indeed bettered. For these fresh peoples had a vigor which Rome had outlived. Nowhere in the world was the Pax Romana in so full flower as in Southern Gaul. In Arlate, in Avenio, in Arusio, Lavinia and Marcus felt that they were in a joyous country—that here they were meeting with something new.

After passing Valentia, Marcus consented to ride together with his sister. He seemed now to need her company. But he was not so talkative nor did he seem to notice the strange sights they were passing. Favonius gave his son certain responsibilities with the new soldiery, and Marcus performed these with thoroughness and decision.

"He's forgotten about the girl," Favonius said to Aurelia. "Strange, Marcus should be so foolish. I don't know what the young men are thinking of these days—falling in love before marriage. We never did it in our day."

Aurelia smiled. "I thought you told me you always cared for me from the very first meeting."

"Well, of course I liked you as I saw you in the family gatherings, but I never thought of loving you until my father told me we were betrothed. Or, indeed, until after our wedding."

"Alas, I was the more deceived," Aurelia teased him. But indeed she was too anxious over Marcus to keep up her banter. Favonius was right. Honorable young Romans did not spend their time love-making.

"It's being out in these provinces," commented Favonius wrathfully. "It makes us forget true Roman ways. Too free—too free."

But Lavinia knew well that Marcus had not forgotten. At Arusio he searched the whole market, the shop booths near the theater, until he found a book-roll containing Euripides' *Ion.*

"I've never been good at Greek," he told Lavinia. "But, by Pollux, I can make this out. Anyone could after seeing it played as at Arlate." Then at Lugudunum Marcus made another search. He kept at it the whole two days they were in the city.

He came to Lavinia with his triumph.

"Well, I found it," he said.

"Found what?" asked Lavinia.

Marcus looked ashamed. "I guess you'll think me a fool buying a musical instrument, when I could no more play it than a donkey."

He lifted it from its box. A lute inlaid with pearl.

"It's just the same size, and it looks like hers—don't you think so?"

"Indeed it does," said Lavinia softly. She touched a string.

"I wish we still had Angelion. He could play it and even some of the tunes if I sang them to him."

"I wouldn't let him touch it," said Marcus strongly, as he put the lute back in its box.

"There was a painting of her in the atrium," he added as if to himself. "If I'd had half a chance, I would have stolen it."

"Oh, Marcus—no."

"Yes, I would. What difference would it make? Her father had been a slave once. We accepted his hospitality and then insulted him. Nice way for guests to act. Might as well steal too."

Marcus' face flushed with shame. He hurried off with his lute to hide it in the baggage.

Lugudunum was the meeting place of many roads. From it the roads ran east, west, south (the road by which Favonius had come), and north, reaching out to the farthest bounds of Gaul and into Germany. The road northward which the Favonian party took was again by a riverside—the River Arar. It passed through Cabillonum, Augustodum, Durocortorum, Noviodunum, and on to the port of Gessoriacum. Strange outlandish names which Lavinia and Marcus tried in vain to pronounce and gave up, laughing. The union of the Celtic original with the Latin ending was surely harsh and inhuman. The inhabitants themselves could not pronounce these towns and were even at this time beginning to soften down the harshness and shorten the names into some sort of music.

At Lugudunum a rain began, and in spite of the fortunate season, the last week in May, it continued with leaden skies and downpours. For these far-southern folk, it was chilly and trying. Aurelia caught cold and kept adding to it in the drafty *raeda*. The inns were of the worst and yet they had to use them. All of the party—even Lavinia and Marcus— were worn out with the long weeks of travel. Lavinia devoted herself to her mother and rode all the while in the curtained *raeda*. She was not willing to leave all duties to the slave, for she saw that her mother was not only ill but unhappy. To have Aurelia unhappy frightened Lavinia, for like her father, she depended upon Aurelia for both courage and wisdom. They saw practically nothing of this northern country and cared less. The days passed in long hours of discomfort and boredom. But at last they entered the port.

"Now, Aurelia *mia*," said Favonius, coming to the *raeda*. "You can thank your stars that the journey is over. Almost over," he amended. "Tomorrow we will be in Britannia."

It was like a shock to Lavinia, a shock of joy and wonder. Tomorrow—Britannia—that far bourne—the farthest of all.

Next morning the embarkation was a clamor which could be heard all over the town. The yells at the mules which would not go aboard. The hoofbeats of rearing and protesting horses; the march of the armed legionary; the shouts of men directing some heavy burden—for the *raedas* and carts as well as the slaves had to be got aboard the barges. Hundreds of such barges were always moored at this busy port. Of these the Favonian party required three. Finally, at about the eighth hour of the day, Favonius summoned Aurelia and Lavinia to come to the ship. Fortunately a suitable vessel was crossing at that time.

"You two will have to make it alone," he said. "Marcus and I must be with the barges to see that all goes well."

CHAPTER THIRTEEN

HE OCEANICUS BRITANNICUS was greatly dreaded by the Romans, especially that part of it called the Fretum Gallicum which lay between this unpronounceable port and the nearest point of Britain. Only Scylla and Charybdis could play such cruel tricks with humans as did these northern waters. The tides ebbing and flowing each day were a wonder to these people of the tideless Mediterranean, and the swift currents of the Fretum played havoc with their small boats.

Lavinia and her mother came out of the inn, into a cold drizzle of rain. They threaded the dirty narrow streets and came to the dock. The ship was not reassuring, piled up with baggage, dirty and unkempt, and as for the rough-bearded sailors, they looked only half human. With no little fear in their hearts Aurelia and Lavinia bade Favonius good-by and stepped aboard. The sailors weighed anchor. They climbed up the ropes like cats and unfurled the queer narrow sail. Hanging at first in folds and flapping helplessly, the sail slowly filled. No moments in the world are so busy as those first of a ship's going. It seemed to come alive as it took up its duty and allied itself with the winds.

Lavinia was unaware that they were moving, but suddenly she grasped her mother's arm.

"How small Father is there on the dock. And those houses—why are they on the other side of the ship?"

Favonius lifted his arm in a gesture of farewell, turned, and walked swiftly away. He had a superstitious fear of watching his wife and daughter as they disappeared on the sea.

The ship, though it looked so uninviting, was really sturdy and strong built—the merchant type, wide and deep. It breasted the currents with less motion and danger than any other sort. It had a high, pointed stern and a stubby ungraceful bow. A railing went all about the deck to guard the cargo. At the stern was a small shelter built of wicker and covered with canvas. Aurelia and Lavinia started toward it.

"How sweet the sea air is after that close inn," Aurelia remarked. She looked with dread toward the shelter where the passengers of all sorts had crowded in.

"Mother, do we have to go there?" asked Lavinia. "The rain has stopped. Can't we stay outside?"

"Yes, daughter, we can," asserted Aurelia. "Have Clotho bring the blankets."

So the two, like two girls together, climbed upon a pile of baggage, wrapped themselves in blankets, and began to look out over the water.

As they did so the sun broke through the clouds. The wide sea flashed into a light steely blue with the twinkling waves running upon it—broad, free, and beautiful. The land behind them was a low purple stretch. In front was only the sea.

Neither Aurelia nor Lavinia had ever before been aboard ship. The vessel was leaping forward with that low whispering sound of sail, almost silent, bird-free. Suddenly both of them were happy. Lavinia felt released—released from the close *raeda,* from the endless roads, the slow jolting of week after week. Released from land itself and the prisonhood of land. No one had ever told her that she must be ill at sea, so the illness did not arrive. Instead came a deep anticipation as if a well of gladness were slowly, slowly filling within her.

Meanwhile the hours went by. Merchant ships were slow. The sun stayed strangely bright. It began to travel toward the horizon but it did not dip below. It only skirted along the rim of the world as if it had no intention of setting.

And now appeared on the far edge of the sea a white cloud. It did not shift but became ever more solid and certain.

"Look, Mother, what a curious whiteness on the edge of the sea," Lavinia said.

Aurelia did not answer. And then Lavinia, turning, saw that her mother's lovely head was bowed low in sleep. Just then a sailor hurried past them. Lavinia pointed to the cloud, questioning, though she knew the man could not understand her.

"Britannia," he answered.

"Britannia!" A deep thrill shook her. She was beholding it. Even though hidden in a cloud. It was there—there! This land that had saved her from a fate that seemed to her now more terrible than death. Trembling, she watched it. Nearer, nearer they came. The cloud did not disperse. Oh, now it was very near and clear to her eyes. She had to see that it was no cloud at all but a sheer cliff, whiter than anything Lavinia had ever seen. Earth was brown. All her life she had known that. Even marble cliffs were gray. Why was this earth of Britain pure white as though it were the lily among lands? The love in her brimmed over. Probably the Britons loved their Britannia but not as Lavinia did now. A great tenderness from her heart went out to it. This land that had saved her. It was receiving her now and it was white, clean in the sunshine after rain, fresh, cold, and clear. Could it be that this young Roman girl was the first among the multitude of those who were to love this land as their very soul?

Now they were coming to the dock. The snow whiteness of the cliff wall soared above them into the sky.

She touched Aurelia's arm to waken her.

"Mother," she whispered, "we are in Britannia and it is as white as a lily flower."

Aurelia was instantly alert. It was no easy thing to find her way in a foreign land without her husband. Where should they go? And she must see where to take her slaves and the baggage. The landing was up a little river which broke its way between two of the chalk cliffs. At the river mouth was a tower that Aurelia knew to be a pharos. The town nestled along the river edge. Aurelia showed none of her anxiety. She directed the slaves at their work, going hither and yon on the deck. Lavinia was not the least help to her. She was still in a dream and followed her mother about like a small child. As they stepped ashore they were met by a stocky Celt.

"*Domina*, we have heard of your coming," he said. "We have rooms for your party ready at our inn. Kindly come this way."

He spoke a perfectly understandable Latin.

Aurelia, Lavinia, and the trail of slaves followed him afoot up the winding street and were soon in the inn yard. The rooms were larger than most inns and, to Aurelia's amazement, clean. And in the room assigned to her and Favonius a brazier was burning.

"Folk is always cold comin' off the sea," said the man with a familiar friendliness no Roman innkeeper would dare use.

"And my wife has the supper warm and ready."

"My husband will be here soon and I'd rather wait for him," answered Aurelia. "But please feed the slaves and give them their quarters."

"Yes, *Domina*—yes, *Domina*. Everything as you wish," said the man. "We knows here how to serve folk. Everybody in Britannia comes here to Dubris sooner or later for a crossin'. And all the merchants from Gaul."

"Your inn is better than most," said Aurelia, who knew how to be kind to those who served her.

The man hurried away. Aurelia inspected Lavinia's cubicle which was next her own.

"I am still tired," she said. "I shall rest in my warm room until your father comes."

Lavinia was never more awake in her life. She was still trembling with intensity. She went with her mother, found the blankets, and wrapped her mother with tender care.

"You are all well, Mother dear?" she questioned.

"Yes, daughter, only so tired after our journey."

Aurelia was almost instantly asleep again.

Lavinia sat down by the brazier. She was restless. She was in Britannia yet enclosed in these four dark walls—seeing nothing, hearing nothing. She went out upon the gallery. Nothing there. Only the innkeeper and his wife bustling about in the courtyard below, and the smell of the cooking filling the air. But Lavinia was not hungry. She was too excited to be hungry. She went down the narrow stairway.

There before her was the wide inn doorway and the street, and on the other side of the street no houses, only the rough hillside and a little crooked path winding up between the bushes. At any other time Lavinia would have realized that she should not go out alone in a strange town, especially a town that was a port. But Britannia did not seem strange to her. All Britannia was her home. Before she realized what she was doing she had left the inn, crossed the street, and was clambering up a path which became ever and ever steeper until it was a sheer breathless climb. On and on she hurried. Suddenly she came out upon the top—suddenly in what seemed a green rolling meadow, greener than any meadow she had ever seen. Only this meadow gave upon space. From this spot she could not behold the sea but she knew that that space was the edge of the cliff and that far below was the ocean.

The sun had set long ago; there was not even any sunset color in the west, but all the meadow and sky were pervaded by a silvery, unearthly brightness such as Lavinia had never seen anywhere—everything in that light was distinct, yet everything was in a dream.

She began to go slowly forward, sensing the loveliness of the place, sensing her own joy and safety. The whole meadow was woven with wild pink roses, trailing in the grass, filling the place with scent, the most delicate personality possessed by any flower. But these lovely roses did not fully possess the air, because they shared it with the freshness of the sea. In hollows were violets almost hidden under leaves. And everywhere along the narrow path were flowers she did not know. Lavinia was very ignorant of open spaces, of the fields and hills. And now that ignorance was a joy to her, because everything was new—new as it is to an awakening child. In the Estrel Mountains she had gathered flowers, but she did not gather them here. She bent down, touching the unknown blossoms with her fingers.

"Flower of Britannia," she would say. "I don't know you but you seem to have knowledge of me."

Now she came to the cliff edge with its abyss and the sea. Far, far along the shore she could see the snow-white capes jutting one after the other into the sea—each crowned with green, each receiving at its foot the leap and roar of spray. Now she could no longer smell the roses but only the sea. Its freedom and strength seemed to enter her. She began to run along the cliff edge with arms outspread. She ran until she was out of breath, and exhausted. Then, laughing, she sank down only to leap up again and run and run and run. Where was the proper, slow-moving Lavinia of the Palatine Hill? She did not even remember her existence. No, no, this was Lavinia of Britain, the new Lavinia.

Now as she ran, she saw a man far away in the meadow hurrying. Yes—it was her father. With arms outspread she ran toward him. She did not notice that his hurry was of wrath. She was too far off to see that his face was a thunder cloud. She only thought that he was Father, here in this beautiful place with her. She ran right to him, threw both arms about his neck.

"Father, Father," she cried, "you have come home too. We are in Britannia."

Never in her life had Lavinia greeted her father this way. All her fear of him was gone. She only loved him.

"What—what in the world!" Favonius disengaged his daughter's arms and gazed at her with astonishment. "What do you mean by coming up here? How dared you to come alone? Don't you know you might have frightened your mother into an illness?"

"Oh, is she frightened? I am sorry, sorry. She seemed so sound asleep. I wrapped her close in her blanket."

"Don't you know," went on Favonius, keeping hold of his wrath with some difficulty, "that you might have tumbled off the cliff? They told me at the inn that many are killed up here every year."

"But, Father, I had no idea of falling over. I was too happy."

"Happy! By the gods, why should you be happy?"

"Oh, to be here—away from Rome—away from the Emperor—away from everything that can hurt us."

"Happy to be here?" he repeated, still amazed.

"Yes—yes. Oh, Father, aren't you happy too? It's our home. It will be our home as long as we live. It belongs to us."

Never for a moment had Favonius thought of Britain other than as a place of exile. This idea was utterly new to him. Now so close to this young vivid daughter of his—he was still holding her hands—he involuntarily caught her spirit, her attitudes of youth.

"Home?" he repeated.

"Yes—oh, Father, it is so—for you, for Mother—for me, most of all."

The thought of home, of freedom, and that he was giving these to his family—all this restored to Favonius a self-respect he was hardly aware of having lost. A sudden sense of comfort and adjustment came over him.

"Well, you're a funny one," he chuckled. "And by Pollux—you're absolutely changed. I believe you look like your mother."

"I—like Mother!" Amazement added to the brightness of Lavinia's eyes. "But Mother is beautiful."

He pinched her cheek. "Well, why shouldn't you be also?"

"Oh—I'm just—not—that's all. That's the reason Decimus—"

She stopped. It seemed a desecration even to pronounce the name of Decimus up here in this beautiful place.

"Decimus should have been flogged," said Favonius, his face reddening.

"No, no, Father—oh, suppose he had not run away!"

"Well, then you would have been a rich married lady in Rome."

"I wouldn't," broke out Lavinia, voicing for the first time something she deeply believed. "I would have been dead."

"Now what do you mean by that, young lady? Weren't you glad to get a husband?" Favonius was still bantering but he saw the bright face of his daughter go dead white and all the joy drain out of it.

"By the gods, did you hate him like that?" he questioned. "Yet you were marrying him."

"I had to," she whispered. "Mother said—"

"Well, what did Mother say?"

Lavinia's lips were dry. She could hardly pronounce the words.

"Mother said—I must bring you and Marcus back to Rome. I was going to try." And again Lavinia's face took on the look of purpose which had so touched Aurelia—long ago. Yes, it seemed long ago in that far off Roman garden.

It is strange how a black oblivion can rest between two minds in one house so they are practically invisible to each other. Such an oblivion had rested between Favonius and his daughter. And at this moment that suddenly melted. Favonius had had no idea that Lavinia was like the person he saw now…He was moved, he was proud. By the gods—the girl was a true Claudian. But above all he was embarrassed.

"Well—well," he said, and then in a lower voice, "Well—well, it's certainly best as it is." Then he added:

"By the way, young lady, are you aware that it is well on to midnight? We must go back to your mother."

"But, Father, it can't be," spoke Lavinia, "perfectly light as it is. Midnight."

"Yes, Britannia is like that. At this time of year there are several nights when there is practically no night at all."

"But why—why?" questioned Lavinia.

"No one knows. In the winter it is just the other way. So they tell me. Most inconvenient."

But Lavinia was entranced.

"Oh no—no, Father, we won't mind darkness in the winter when we're in the house anyway. I'd pay anything for this wonderful silver light."

She looked about her. The light had scarcely decreased since she had run up the hill from the inn. And now she remembered that this day had begun long ago in Gaul and the day was still with them.

"But why isn't it the same in Gaul?" she inquired.

"It is almost. Only you did not notice it on account of the cloudiness and rain. The folk here are afraid of these white nights. They say the ghosts come out."

But even this did not dampen Lavinia's ardor. "Maybe they're good ghosts."

"We'll hope so," smiled Favonius.

They took hands and began to walk slowly toward the town.

"Father," asked Lavinia, standing stock still in the path, "where is the gulf?"

"The gulf? Do you mean the Fretum Gallicum?"

"Oh no—the great gulf at the world's edge where you'd tumble down among stars."

Favonius laughed.

"It's here in Britannia, isn't it?" she questioned.

"No, daughter."

"But Mother said Britannia was on the very edge of the world. It seems like it with this funny daylight."

"Well," said Favonius seriously, "of course there is such a gulf somewhere. The earth must come to an end and have an edge. But it isn't here."

"Does anybody know where it is?"

"No—not even the bravest mariner, but all are afraid of it."

"I'd love to see it," declared Lavinia.

"Nonsense. You certainly would not," responded her father.

"Do you know," he went on informatively, "the Greeks have a theory that the world is round. Just like a ball. Foolishness, of course. Hundreds of years ago there used to live an old Greek, quite near where we had our Villa Velia. He was one of them who believed the world was round and used to try to prove it by the stars."

Lavinia went into gales of laughter. She was happy anyway—and this was vastly amusing.

"Yes," went on her father, "round as a ball, and just hanging in the air. I have a great respect for the Greeks but they surely have a crazy streak in them—a crazy streak."

They began to clamber down the steep path to the town of Dubris. As they did so, it occurred to Favonius what a queer conversation this was to be holding with his daughter Lavinia. Ancient philosophies and the formation of the world. The girl was growing up.

Just as they entered the narrow street, the kindled fire flashed up from the pharos, high above them on the opposite cliff. But even at this late hour, the ships on the white twilight sea did not need this Roman lighthouse to kindle its fire.

Chapter Fourteen

T DUBRIS next morning appeared a centurion sent from the north to take charge of the Iberian soldiers. He marched them off early as if there might be some special need of them on the frontier. Just as Aurelia had foretold, they parted from Favonius with great show of devotion, brandishing spears and banging them against their shields with terrible clangor. Those who passed nearest Favonius spoke heartily.

"See you in the north, General. We'll see you soon."

"I hope so," responded Favonius, but he did not really hope so. He had been thrust into a judge's position here in Britain and had been robbed of his soldierhood. And he wished with all his heart he were going with the company. He observed one thing with pleasure.

"See you again, Little General. See you again."

The soldiers were shouting this at Marcus with even more affection than they showed to Favonius. The boy had a gift with men. Yes, undoubtedly, a gift of leadership.

The Claudian party did not get started until noontime.

A small party now, only the family and slaves—missing the confusion and tread of the soldiers. It was raining a fine mist. Lavinia and her mother rode in the *raeda*. The pedestrian slaves wrapped themselves in cloaks. Favonius and Marcus were on horseback. And finally Lavinia begged so earnestly to ride on Triga that her mother at last consented.

"I can't imagine why you are so eager," she commented. "There is nothing to see."

The sun came out with a glitter on green leaves and greener meadows. Lavinia hastened to her place beside Marcus. No sooner had they cleared the little town than the whole party from Favonius to the meanest slave was aware that they were in a new land.

Northern Gaul had been a rude land as compared with the south but this Britain was ruder still. They were almost at once in deep forest. The road which had started singing like a melody at the Roman gate sang here under the silent trees. But everywhere one sensed the island quality aloof from the world.

As these folk moved forward in their new land, each soul of them was separated like a star in space, each in an orbit all his own. Even what they saw was different, as if they looked each on some different realm. To Favonius this Britain was the place of an unfriendly governor, of an unfriendly work which he was sure to do ill. To Aurelia it was a homeless forest where she must try to create a home for her family.

As for Marcus, he was not seeing the forest nor the white Roman road; his heart had gone north with the soldiers. Yes, Marcus could be a soldier in this land—his dearest wish. No foolishness about marching up and down in city streets, or forts where fort was not needed. Even in Gaul he'd heard about these frontiers of Britain. There were wild men here who always must be reconquered—men half naked and painted blue, dirty creatures who fought like wolves. Oh, there was something to put one on his mettle. It was worth while.

And Lavinia—she was still so possessed by anticipation that she had no room for criticism of anything. Her mood was that of a very young child who takes all happenings as inevitable and right because they happen. Did it rain in Britain? Then that was Britain's way. Did the sun never set? That also was natural. Did the wheat stay unripe long after harvest season? Well, then it looked pretty so green and waving. For no reason at all, a mist of joy settled down over the morning. It was a quality of infancy which Lavinia was never to lose. People who have it can become either poets or saints. But Lavinia was neither at present.

The party made easy day trips to Durovernum, to Durobrivis. At both places they were entertained by Roman citizens, ex-soldiers who were proud to have a Claudian family under their roof.

Their third stop was Londinium.

"We are now approaching their metropolis," said Claudius Favonius, not without a sneer.

The road became crowded. All sorts of people—going to market, bringing produce to the Londinium ships. Lavinia was constantly laughing.

"Oh, look at that funny man with the bright striped garment on his legs. We saw trousers in the Gallic mountains, but not like that."

And Marcus laughing too. "But wait, wait for that one with the long red hair. Do you suppose he ever washed it? And his beard and mustache and all the rest of it. He might as well be a goat."

And Lavinia: "Look at that poor woman with the seven children at her heels. She strides along like a lively pony and the children too."

Yes, they were certainly strong folk, these Britons. They looked as if nothing could kill them. In this region there were many fine fields, for Britain was famous for its wheat and barley. But there were also stretches where the land was very low—a spongy bog—and the road had to be built up a high causeway. Slow little streams meandered through it. The road crossed these on wooden bridges. Now they came to the shore of the wide tidal river, Thamisis. They followed it upstream to where it suddenly narrowed. Here was another wooden bridge which they crossed.

At the end of the bridge was a great Roman gate. They were in Londinium.

"What a queer city!" said Marcus. "It looks as if it grew up by chance."

"And so it did," responded Favonius. "It is a city of merchants, traders, and ship owners."

The streets were crowded with men from the world over—Arabs, Syrians, Phoenicians, Iberians, Gauls, all mingled with the Romans. Every sort of garment was here, from the Roman toga to the long Oriental cloak. The center of town was handsome and Roman built, but from there it stretched over the low ground in every direction, warehouses, homes, huts of every description. Favonius and Marcus were amazed at its size—as big as Lugudunum but in no wise so handsome. The same little streams which had wandered through the swamps wandered through the city.

Favonius learned that Falco, the governor, was at this time in London. He called upon him to receive orders and returned to Aurelia both puzzled and troubled.

"Falco says I am to take charge of certain judicial matters in Isca Salurem," he told his wife.

"And where is that?" she inquired.

"On the very edge of civilization," he answered gloomily. "Out beyond Glevum, wherever that may be. It is a military fort and stronghold in the country of the Silurian tribes. No fit place for you to live, Aurelia."

"But isn't there a city near? I certainly want to be with you."

"No, the near-by settlement, Venta, is no more than a *kanaba,* lived in by the hangers-on of the legion. I certainly will not have you there."

"But where then?" she asked desperately.

"I don't know yet. Falco says there are good cities not far, Glevum, for instance. I'll establish you and the children there. Anyway, the governor says I am not to be long in one place. I shall flit about at his bidding."

This was hard news to hear.

"Perhaps he is only trying you out to find what best suits you," said Aurelia to encourage Favonius, but her own heart was heavy in her breast.

From Londinium they journeyed southwest through the country of the Atrebates.

The country before reaching Londinium had been wild, but this was far wilder. For miles the road passed through forest swamps, splendid oak, ash, and beech of which both trunk and branches were filmed with green moss as though they had never been dry from one century to the next. In the frequent drizzles of rain this moss became intensely green. From the cleared space of the Roman road, the travelers looked either side into a night-like gloom. Flowers by the roadside bloomed in profusion. And wherever it could find space or sunlight the hawthorn was bride-white, filling the air with a freshness as of the youth of the world.

Sometimes the forest would be broken—though scarcely broken by a native village. The huts huddled together like the lairs of animals. Most of the huts were round, of beehive shape, made of wattles and earth; some were pits with a low roof for covering. "Slummy towns," Marcus called them as they passed.

There were hours of deep silence sometimes broken by the cry of an unfamiliar bird, sometimes by stirrings in the forest. Marcus would whisper,

"Look at that fat old bear rooting at the foot of that tree."

Later they both saw an elk drinking at a stream, his huge antlers bent over the water. How he crashed away through the forest when he heard them approach! They crossed the upper Thamisis but not on a bridge. Here were only flat stones and some of them not visible. The water reached over the hubs of the *raeda*.

Lavinia crossed on Triga who had to swim the mid-stream. She was thrilled when the hoof steps beneath her ceased and the curious rhythmic motion of swimming began. Of course she was soaked and had to resort to the curtained *raeda* for a complete change.

"But I swam," she kept saying delightedly. "I swam on a horse."

"It seems to me it was Triga did the swimming," remarked Aurelia. "Daughter, you act as if you were only seven years old instead of a young woman."

She threw both arms about her mother's neck and kissed her.

"Perhaps I am. Oh, Mother, it's so strange. I don't feel old and grown up the way I did in Rome."

Not for worlds would Aurelia have laid her own burden of sorrow on her daughter.

Marcus, too, had his adventure, a foolish one and a dangerous one. He was riding at the edge of the road when he heard a sound of grunting and twigs breaking. There, not ten feet from the paved way, was a group of wild pigs contentedly rooting the damp soil. Marcus whipped his sword from its scabbard and leaped down from the roadway into the forest.

The pigs scattered, squealing with fright, but Marcus gave chase. Fortunately his pony had not forgotten its wild skill and went scampering over roots and boggy soil. Trogus leaped his horse into the forest, shouting:

"Young master! come back, come back!"

And Favonius, horrified, leaped after Trogus.

But Marcus would not stop. Never had he had such sport. If he only had a spear he could get that fat old boar lumbering along in the rear of the herd. Suddenly the said old boar turned, stood ground, and in an instant had sprung against the pony's chest, using his tusks with deadly skill. The pony shrieked and reared. And in that moment Marcus, true to his military training, leaned down almost to the horse's belly and slashed the boar deep with the sword. Here came Trogus shouting, expostulating, sputtering, but he finished the boar just as it was making another furious lunge. Here came Favonius swearing with anxiety.

"Great gods, Marcus! you know nothing of boar hunting. Did you never hear that boar is the most dangerous animal? A bear is nothing to it. You mustn't be so city-bred."

"But look, Father, we got him, we got him!" Marcus was too elated with hunter triumph to care what his father said.

"Sheer luck, son. Now don't let me hear of any such foolishness again. Get back to the road. Look how Ventus is bleeding."

Back to the road they clambered. Two slaves went into the forest and slung the boar's carcass on a pole. They could hardly carry it to the road. There they swung the pole across two much-distressed and protesting horses, while Marcus ran about directing everything. Lavinia must come and look; Aurelia must get out of the *raeda* and look; everybody must look at the boar.

Trogus, who knew well who had really killed the boar and averted catastrophe, said nothing. That is, he only talked to Ventus. Washing the wound on Ventus' chest, pouring on the liniment, he kept muttering:

"Never mind, old fellow. You're safe now. Thanks to *somebody*. We won't say who, old fellow. Oh no. We won't say who. Somebody ran him through, that old boar. You wouldn't be here, old fellow; Young Master wouldn't be here—oh no."

Favonius, passing near and overhearing the one-sided conversation, gave Trogus a look that was almost a wink; and Trogus knew that he was not to be without his reward.

Chapter Fifteen

ALLEVA was reached on the noon of the third day. A large town and prosperous. Its wall was twenty feet high, its gate imposing, with two arches. Favonius was so pleased with it that he wanted to leave his family here, but Aurelia begged so earnestly to be set nearer to his destination that at last he yielded. They were entertained by a Celtic family who lived in a large house near the Forum. Aurelia was so weary that she could hardly thank her hostess for her kindness.

"Oh, it's the swamp fever ye have," said the simple woman. "We all get it at first. I'll give ye my herb drink."

And Aurelia drank the bitter draft and went off to sleep, not even eating the festive supper which the generous Celts provided.

Next day the party went slowly onward. All were weary of the unending trail; not only Aurelia, but every slave longed to find the destination and settle down. Only Marcus and Lavinia still looked with interest at the passing scene. The droves of wild horses brought down from the hills, the rude wooden houses with peaked roofs, log cabins, typical then of the frontier as they are today. Then the travelers took a British crossroad to the Fosse Way—the great road which led from the north—and pursuing this, came at last to Corinium.

This city, strange to say, was almost as large as Londinium itself. It was the capital of the district—its walls measured miles around. Outside of the walls was a space cleared by the Romans—as always—for safety. Beyond this, amid charming wooded mountains, were suburban homes. The travelers went to a *mansio* where Aurelia sought her bed, too weary even to sleep. Favonius called Marcus and Lavinia to go out with him to see the city. They easily found their way, for Corinium had been laid out by the Romans checkerboard fashion. In the center was a stone basilica more than three hundred feet long, a splendid Forum with columns, space for the citizens to trade and barter and have their councils in the open air, but also many protected rooms where they could meet in winter weather. The three were walking in the sunny Forum when an old man called them and overtook them. They did not know him at first he was so lively. It was Icinus, the old Celtic slave whom Favonius had brought from Rome and allowed to ride with Marcus.

"Oh, master, master," he cried out, "ye have come to my own country. My own mountains. My little town was only a few miles from here. It's gone to naught, because all the folk have moved here to the city. My brother Zennor, my old neighbor Bodmin. I've met 'em both, master, and they knew me and were not ashamed of me."

"Well, that's good indeed," responded Favonius. He was not sorry to make such connection, for he trusted this old man perhaps above all his slaves.

"An', master—I saw somethin' I want to show ye."

The old man's voice changed to a humble pleading tone so

familiar to a slave owner. Favonius knew he was about to ask a favor.

"Just across the Forum yonder," Icinus went on. "A notice of a house for sale. It's a man died. My brother told me—an' his wife and children is goin' back to Gaul where her folks live. She's asellin' the place for nothin'."

They followed the old man across the beautifully paved square to where a fluttering parchment was nailed to the wall of the colonnade.

Favonius read it carefully.

"Where is this?" he asked.

"Just outside the gate where country houses begins. Ye could walk there, master."

"All right, lead us there."

The old man limped ahead of them, not able to hurry fast enough for his wish.

Favonius was to be stationed within easy distance of this city, Corinium. Might this not be the place for his home?

They followed the old man out the city gate across the cleared meadow to the house in question. The place was surrounded by a high stone wall. They knocked at the double gate and were admitted. The whole place was utterly different from anything they had known in Rome. They found themselves in a grassy space bordered on three sides by the colonnade of the house. The space had many flowers, and a straight path led from the gate to the central door of the house.

Here the sad-voiced widow met them—very eager to sell them her home, yet hating to show it to strangers.

"Where is the atrium?" inquired Favonius.

"We have no atrium, sir," said the widow. "An atrium is so cold with the open compluvium and the pool. We have our garden instead, and here in the tablinium we live in winter and cool days. The altar, you see, is there and the little window is glassed. The big window has thick wooden shutters for cold days. But it's to the south and we can have it open all summer."

She led the way to the open window where was a splendid view of valley and little stream, the headwaters of the Thamisis, and magnificent oaks showed in the afternoon light.

"Oh, Father, how lovely!" cried Lavinia, leaning on the sill. "Oh, it's prettier than any villa in Italy."

She looked back at the widow whose eyes were filling with tears. Lavinia impulsively touched her hand.

"My husband loved this view," said the widow. "He was half Roman and he always loved views. He had the house set specially so we could see this."

"He was wise," said Favonius kindly. "Rest assured, madame, if we buy your house we will appreciate his wisdom and taste."

The little woman dashed the tears out of her eyes with the back of her hand.

"There, there," she said, "I shouldn't be so foolish. I'll be glad to sell my home. Then I can go to my father in Gaul an' he'll take care of the children."

She began to show them the house.

"We're leaving the big braziers," she told them. "And this room is always warm. So are all these rooms on the east side. They are heated with the hypocaust and so are the three rooms of the bath." The house was one room, deep shaped like a letter U, with the garden in the middle. The woman led them upstairs where the second story was built of wattle and daub and had many windows. Houses in Italy looked inward; this house of Britain looked outward on the wood and field and made every effort to catch the sun.

She led them outside and showed them the hypocaust furnace, buried in a pit. This was a marvel to Marcus and Lavinia. Of course hypocausts were known for public baths in Rome, but they had had no such luxury in the old-fashioned home on the Palatine.

"Madame," said Favonius at parting, "if my wife will consent to stay in Corinium, I shall buy your house tomorrow afternoon."

Aurelia did consent. Indeed, she was too worn out to go a mile further. Besides, she liked Corinium among the hills, so different from the low cities of the plain. The widow whose name was Vilbia invited them to stay with her until she could make ready and move away. Aurelia was given the best sunny bedroom. The slaves were crowded in with Vilbia's slaves.

Favonius prepared to go onward to his post. The parting of husband and wife in the strange land was a hardship they could hardly face with courage.

"I shall be back next month," he told Aurelia. "Besides, I am leaving Creticus with you. He is a swift horseman and faithful and will carry messages between us. You are to rest. To do nothing else. Lavinia and Marcus may as well take hold. They are old enough and I shall command them."

In all the British journey, so carefree for themselves, Marcus and Lavinia had been completely oblivious of the anxiety and tragedy of their elders. Even now they only half sensed it, such is the gulf between the young and old. But when their father led them out into the garden for the last talk together they had to see some of it.

"The gods know," said Favonius, "I would not leave

your mother if I did not have to. I must go. Now the whole responsibility is with you. You two must establish our new home. But most of all you must care for your mother. Take all the burden that would naturally be hers. You can do it if you really care about it. If when I come back your mother is worse I shall thrash both of you. Depend upon it—I shall."

Marcus blushed scarlet. He knew his father would make good his threat. Military discipline was natural to him, and Roman discipline also.

"All right, Father," Marcus managed to answer. "You won't have to thrash us. We can do what you want."

"And, Lavinia," said Favonius. "I was much pleased with you in Northern Gaul. You really cared for your mother all the way. But since we have been in Britannia you have been neglectful and let Clotho do everything. I want that changed."

Lavinia was frightened. She was also ashamed. She knew what her father said was true. She could not answer a word.

"I am taking ten of the slaves," went on Favonius. "I shall need that many men to make safe the journey. You may have to buy several slaves. I am leaving the funds in your hands, Marcus. Vilbia will help you in many things. But do not buy any of her slaves."

Lavinia looked her wonder.

"Yes, Vilbia is kind and trustworthy, but she would not be human if she did not palm off an old useless slave or two when she has the long journey to go. On the other hand, you must listen to Vilbia in the matter of making friends."

"Oh, we won't bother about friends," said Marcus importantly. "We'll be too busy."

"No, you may not. But friends will bother about you. They seem to think here in Britannia that a Claudian is little lower than the gods. They'll want to meet you. You'll have to choose. Ask Vilbia. She's a good woman and has a fine reputation in the town. See that your mother is quiet. The doctor here—heaven knows whether he is any good—says absolute rest is necessary."

Next morning, after a half-hour alone with Aurelia, Favonius came out to the gate where the horses and slaves awaited him. Marcus and Lavinia, too, were waiting. Favonius kissed his son and daughter on the forehead.

"You can ask Trogus questions about most things," he said. "Farewell."

He put one foot on the horse block, sprang on his horse, and went clattering away, followed by his slaves.

Marcus looked at Lavinia—both their faces were solemn and a little pale.

"Now," said Marcus, "now it's up to us."

Chapter Sixteen

LAVINIA hurried to her mother. She found her lying on a couch, not weeping save that tears kept filling her eyes and brimming over.

Lavinia put both arms about her. "Don't cry, Mother. Marcus and I are with you."

Marcus had followed and was standing at the foot of the couch.

"I am not afraid for us, daughter. It's your father. He is so fiery, and if he offends people here—well, they might murder him."

"Oh, Father's all right," spoke Marcus. "And now that he has so much to do, he'll feel a lot better. He hated the traveling. Besides"—Marcus came around the couch and took his mother's hand—"besides, if Father doesn't show up as soon as you expect, I'll go and fetch him."

Clotho came in preparing to send the young folks out of the sick room.

"Clotho," said Lavinia, "go and get your mistress some warm milk and some of that fresh-cracked barley we had this morning, and honey. I think she will eat it now."

Clotho flounced out of the room. Aurelia looked her wonder at these two changed children of hers. What must Favonius have done to them?

So wondering, she ate her breakfast for the first time since coming to Corinium.

It was a week before Vilbia could get away. Sure enough, she did try to sell several of her slaves, especially a tottering old man who worked in the garden.

"He looks weak," she told Marcus, "but he can do much work. And any flower will grow if he does but touch it. I'll let you have him for a few sesterces."

"No," said Marcus, very businesslike. "We'll just have to decide later about the slaves."

"It will break his heart to leave the garden, especially now in June," said Vilbia, shaking her head.

At the last moment she gave the old man to Marcus. Marcus was not sure he wanted him even as a gift.

Then at last they were all gone—mistress, children, slaves, horses, and baggage. The place was empty, free for Marcus and Lavinia to settle in it.

"The first thing to do is to scrub the house from top to bottom," commanded Lavinia. "Vilbia did not keep house the way we did at home."

"Dindia's strong enough to do it," observed Marcus. "And Xeno and Facilis can help her."

Lavinia shook her head. "Dindia is only cook, as you know. If I ask her to scrub, I'll never hear the last of it. Mother, of course, could command her, but she'd only spill things around and do it wrong to spite me. Don't you remember we left Fabiola in Rome? She always saw to the scrubbing."

Marcus did not deny this. He knew that what Lavinia said

was true. Each slave to his own duty. And it was a very misery to try to change them.

"Well, I'll have to get a woman in the market. You go with me, Lavinia, and—yes, I'll take Trogus too."

It was early morning when Marcus and Lavinia started out. This city was to be their home. They viewed it eagerly. Yes, it was laid out checkerboard fashion as were all the Roman colony cities, but it was not filled in Roman fashion. The houses were set this way and that—not facing the streets; all had gardens, and everywhere were broad open spaces, golden with buttercups or daisies. And the dew was not yet burned off. No houses were old like those in Rome. Everything was in good repair.

"It's a queer city," said Marcus. "It's as much meadows and hills as city."

"It's a nice city," Lavinia gave a little skip. "It looks good and it smells good. But the people are funny."

"They're a great mix-up," agreed Marcus. "Almost as bad as Londinium."

They came again to the large basilica and paved Forum, passed that and entered the unpaved market, twice as big as Forum and basilica together. It was filled with booths and vendors and buyers as noisy as a circus before the game.

"Pots from Gaul—just off the ship."

"Horses—wild horses, broken horses; take your choice, choice, choice."

> "Cloaks and togas
> Red and blue
> All for you
> All for you. . . ."

Marcus and Lavinia could not begin to understand all the

cries, though many of them changed suddenly from wild Gallic into Latin as the two came near. But even the Latin was queerly broken and nasal.

> "Slaves from Ivernia
> Best in the land
> Here they stand—
> Horsehides—cowhides—cured and slick
> Take your pick
> Take your pick."

"There are the slaves over there," said Marcus. "Come." And he took Lavinia's hand to lead her toward the corner of the square.

It was a strange display—men and women standing to be sold as if they were cattle. A row of slave blocks on which young vigorous men were mounted. On one of these stood a young woman—or was she some sort of a faun? She was clad in black horsehide—but underneath the chancy garment she stood like a buxom caryatid who might hold up a cornice.

But no Greek caryatid would have associated with her. Her hair, black, long, and matted, fell to her waist. Her face was one blank despair seeing nothing—eyes of intense blue and deeply shadowed by long black lashes. Trogus pointed his finger.

"There's the scrub woman for ye," he said.

"Oh, but she's so terribly, terribly dirty," complained Lavinia.

"Nevertheless, young mistress, she'll make places clean. That kind work like devil spirits. They come from an island west of Britannia. There's nothin' like 'em."

"I like her too," declared Marcus. He turned to the trader and asked the price.

"Four hundred sesterces," said the man.

"Too much. Why do you talk nonsense to me?"

Of course, Marcus knew that this drama of give and take must be played through. What was the fun of bargaining if you did not complain of the price? He and Trogus withdrew to whisper together. Lavinia stood wondering at the strange wild creature. Now Marcus came back, stating his price. The trader clapped his hands and wept.

"Why has a Roman come to make me a beggar in the streets?" he cried.

Meanwhile Trogus pointed to a young boy on a block at the other end.

"There's another good one," he said. "You might get a price on both of them."

"Why not get that third one too?" Marcus said. "We need a stable boy."

"Gods, no, young master. Two Ivernians could run away with your whole house. Three would spell disaster."

"What do you mean, Trogus?"

"You'll see—you'll see, young master," laughed Trogus.

The slave woman had not seemed even to be aware of Marcus and Lavinia. But the moment Trogus pointed to the boy she leaped from the block and, though her ankles were chained, crawled on hands and knees to Marcus and snatched at his hands, kissing them and uttering the strangest keen wail like mourners at a bier.

Marcus, horrified, leaped away from her. But then just as quickly she crawled to Lavinia, clasping her hands with a grasp which Lavinia could in no wise loosen, kissing them and pleading in her strange tune-like words. Lavinia tried to free her hands, but now those brimming blue eyes were gazing fixedly on hers, and pity welled up in Lavinia's heart before she knew it. After all, Lavinia was like her mother in her kindness to all creatures.

"What is she saying?" Lavinia demanded of the trader. "No—no, leave her alone." For the trader had darted forward and was jerking the woman away.

"It's all about that boy at the far end. He's her brother. We caught 'em both at the riverside, rompin' together like a couple o' colts. She seems to love him like a bear loves its cubs."

Lavinia began to talk to the woman just as if she could understand.

"Don't cry—don't cry. We'll buy you both. Yes, Marcus, please buy both of them. I'm sure they're what we want."

Lavinia completely spoiled the bargaining for, of course, the trader was well aware that the sale was sure. At last it was effected. Marcus paid the man in Roman coin and received in change some Gallic coin and two make-believe swords of iron.

"What on earth are these?" he demanded.

"That's old British money," said the man. "But it's good. Ye can spend it."

As for the slave woman, she was suddenly still. Her blue, blue eyes roved from one face to another, trying to comprehend the sale. She seemed holding her breath. When she saw the money passed she gave a guttural cry.

"Take off her shackles," commanded Lavinia.

But Trogus objected: "Now, now, young mistress, not so fast. She'll run away sure."

"Well, then let her. Look—you wouldn't let a horse's ankles be chained like that and all bleeding."

Trogus knelt down and broke the chain with a stone. "Young Mistress is gettin' a bossy way with her," he muttered.

For a moment it seemed as if he had been right, for the woman snatched the stone from his hand, ran the length of the slave booth—but there she fell on her knees before her brother and broke his chains as her own had been broken. Then she threw both arms about him in a passion of weeping which could be heard all over the market.

"Gods, she's a queer one," spoke the embarrassed Marcus. But Lavinia in spite of herself felt the tears running down her own cheeks. After a few minutes she went to the woman and shook her arm.

"That's enough now," she ordered. "Be still, we're going home."

To her astonishment the woman was instantly still and turned to follow her, grasping her brother by the hand.

"Does she understand Latin?" Lavinia asked the trader.

"No, mistress—not a word but her own pig talk. Her name's Buvinda. We named her after the river. And the boy's named Gorm."

By this time the little party was extremely conspicuous —everybody looking. But Buvinda and Gorm walked on soberly enough.

At another part of the market Marcus paid out two of the iron swords for some fuller's earth. This was to help Buvinda with her cleaning.

At the house Lavinia found Dindia all honey and cream. She was perfectly aware that her mistress had bought a slave rather than ask her to do this chore.

"I'll teach her, young mistress. When I heard ye was comin' back I had Facilis draw a kettle full of water from the well there by the gate, an' it's startin' to heat over a big fire in front o' the stables outside."

"That's good, Dindia. But, Vesta help us, we've got to wash

her first. Mother will be horrified at such a dirty slave."

"All right, young mistress, all right." Dindia seized Buvinda's hand to drag her along. But Buvinda gave her a staggering cuff on the ear and turned to Lavinia with a volley of remonstrance.

"Buvinda, you must not do that. Come now. You must do what Dindia tells you. Come and wash."

Then like a lamb the Ivernian woman followed. Only she kept strong hold of her brother all the way. She seemed utterly puzzled when Dindia brought a bowl of hot water and Lavinia, dipping her own hands and face, showed her she must do likewise. However, she imitated quickly, bursting into laughter when she found the water warm, sloshing her face, her neck, her arms—then bringing her brother to the dirty water, utterly puzzled again when it appeared that Gorm must have clean water of his own for washing. Lavinia could but note how fair was Buvinda's skin under its coat of filth.

Soon the pails of hot water were ready.

"Begin on the farthest rooms of the bath," commanded Lavinia. "When she has learned there we'll let her attack the tablinium."

She hurried on to Aurelia's room. Whatever Lavinia did her first thought was to tell Aurelia about it. For Mother was always so interested—so merry if it was a joke, so sorrowful if it were sad. Aurelia listened doubtfully to the recital.

"Oh dear, I wish I could have gone with you," she said. "I fear you have a wild Maenid on your hands who will only make trouble with everybody."

She had scarcely finished when running steps came along the outside corridor and into the room. There was Dindia, her hair down, her tunic wet, her face a cloud of wrath.

"Come, young mistress. Please come. We can't do a thing with her. She dashes the water all over the floor. She won't touch the fuller's earth. She's got the slave boys all laughing and not one of 'em will turn a hand."

But here were more running steps, noisier than the first, and here was Buvinda, soaked with the water from head to toe, her blue eyes flashing, her hands gesturing with a pantomime that showed the whole scrubbing scene and how impossible and foolish was all scrubbing. She addressed Lavinia with a torrent of words. Then she saw Aurelia—perhaps something in Lavinia's horrified look made her realize that Aurelia must not be disturbed, that she was ill and must be quiet. For Buvinda changed utterly, instantly, knelt on the pavement by the couch stroking Aurelia's bare feet, then her hands, crooning some word of affection and repentance, and gazing at her face as if completely fascinated with Aurelia's delicate beauty.

Aurelia's laughter pealed through the room.

"Lavinia dear—you certainly have bought a Maenid, or maybe she is the nymph of some leaping fountain that never ceases. Oh, my dear, however will you teach her anything?"

"Come—come—leave Mother alone," cried Lavinia despairingly. "Oh, Mother, has she hurt you?"

"No, no, child. She has given me healthy laughter. Take her along and the gods be with you."

So Lavinia led the repentant Buvinda back to the farthest room of the bath. The floor was streaming. Lavinia showed her how to take the water up with a ladle, how to mop it dry and leave it fresh and shining. Then on to the tepidarium and to the caldarium, then to a bedroom. Never in all the service of Buvinda, now and later, was Lavinia to know how it was possible for her to understand Lavinia as if Latin were clear to her mind. It seemed an instinct born of her complete devotion. But she could never understand other people no matter how they insisted. Now she was proud when the rooms were washed to Lavinia's liking, though time and again she shook her head, as if wondering what in the wide world her mistress could want with this multitude of strangely furnished rooms.

Chapter Seventeen

NEXT MORNING Lavinia wakened with a sense of release and happiness. Responsibility was new to her and was like a tonic to her soul. Out in the sunny corridor she met Marcus, fresh dressed from the bath.

"I'm fixing a corner of the garden by the fishpool for Mother," said Marcus. "It's a grand place with bushes and flowers, and Vilbia's old gardener is doing wonders with it."

Lavinia did not trust to Dindia this time but herself led Buvinda with the slave boys carrying pails of steaming water to the tablinium. It was a beautiful room, large and well spaced; not only did it have the generous window toward the meadow, but an arched door leading to the front. Here Lavinia hoped to hang some rich curtains from home.

But what amazed Buvinda was the floor. She gazed at it half in fear, then fell on hands and knees to examine it closely. When Lavinia walked across it Buvinda uttered a little scream of remonstrance. How could one so offend the gods? For the floor was tessellated mosaic, white, red, green, blue, all bright colors. And within a great circle in the center was a picture of Orpheus playing his lyre and drawing all animals to his spell. Lambs, deer, little hares amid tufts of grass, and birds perched in a tree.

Now Buvinda was all reverence and awe. She touched the hares, the birds; with soft caressing words she touched the lyre, humming a swift tune. But she did not touch Orpheus. Animals she knew; harps and music she knew; gods she knew, but she had never seen them thus stand forth to mortal sight.

"Come, come, Buvinda," urged Lavinia. "We must have the whole room washed quickly. I want it ready for Mother by noon."

But would Buvinda throw steaming hot water on a god? She would not, nor would she wash his face as if he were a mortal. There was reason in all things and this was not reasonable. No commands could force her. In the end Dindia had to wash the floor while Buvinda tenderly went over the painted walls where wheat and flowers made a pattern. And this she did with as delicate a touch as the delicate painting required.

They had scarcely finished when Marcus came in to direct the setting of the altar. The slaves carried it in, took it from its case, set it on a marble table. They chose the same south corner as had been the use in Rome. Then Marcus and Lavinia lifted the images one by one, placing them under the marble canopy exactly in the order as they had always been. *Penates*, god of the cupboard, the dancing god pouring libation, the bearded ancestor. They brought a lamp and lighted it.

"Oh," breathed Lavinia. "It is home. It is exactly like home."

"Yes," said Marcus. "But I think we ought to have a god from right around here. It's safer."

"What god?" questioned Lavinia.

"Oh, I don't know their names. But there were some in the

market. I saw them. Come—you help me choose."

So with Trogus to carry burdens they set out again for the market. This time it was not quite so noisy. The first hours of ardent buying were over. There was more room to move around. The image booth was the largest of all. It was set forth with images of all sorts. Many Jupiters, Jupiter Optimus Maximus, he was called, yet still more images of Mars, and cupboard images. Everyone had to have one of those, else how would the larder be kept full? These were crude, but yet cruder were the native gods.

"Who is this?" asked Marcus, pointing to a small man image.

"That's Nodens, young master. He's the special god around here and all the way up to Glevum and beyond. Very powerful."

"Ought we get that?" Marcus consulted Lavinia.

"He's terribly ugly."

"Yes, but all the more reason to have him. He might get angry if he is special here and we neglect him."

"All right," she agreed. "But then how about that strange one with the stag antlers on his head? Perhaps he's lord of the forests."

"Indeed he is, mistress. And when the winds get to raging in the trees and snow flies everywhere there's no one so powerful as this here."

So a statue of the forest god went into the basket.

On the same booth were votive images of hares, pigs, and deer, little magic hands and a swastica from the Orient, and piles of magic nails. These could be driven into a wall with the saying:

"Thus do I nail an evil stomachache, a dread disease, an accident to my enemy."

The man gathered up a handful.

"These are cheap. Better have some in case o' need."

"No, no," said Marcus, "I have no enemies in Britannia."

"You're lucky," laughed the man.

The next booth sold amulets and jewelry. Lavinia, being feminine, moved on toward it, fascinated. There were twisted rings of silver made by the native Britons, beautiful silver broaches of the safety-pin pattern. These, too, were native. And a gold chain from Gaul with an exquisite golden wheel and a crescent. The dealer quickly threw it about Lavinia's neck.

"See, mistress, the crescent is in the front and the wheel in the back. That's the moon and the sun so you're sure of luck from one or the other."

Lavinia fingered it lovingly.

"You look pretty in that," observed Marcus. And Lavinia blushed at the compliment. It was nice for Marcus to think her pretty for any cause.

"See here, Lavinia, I'm going to get that for you."

Lavinia virtuously took it off.

"How foolish, Marcus. I have an amulet already. And this one is of gold."

The man instantly named a price. Much lower than Marcus expected. Followed an animated argument, price and counterprice. And finally Marcus proudly paid just half of the original sum and affectionately threw the chain about his sister's neck.

After this they must needs buy sacrificial cakes for the altar, lettuce and leeks which showed themselves temptingly fresh, a great jar of olive oil which the dealer's slave carried for them, a small jar of British wine. It must be confessed that the purse which Favonius had given his son was much slenderer than that son had quite expected.

At home they hastened to deck the altar and set out the new images. Cena, which here in Britain was served at midday, came steaming upon the table, and Marcus and Lavinia went to fetch their mother.

Aurelia had hoped to have her dinner quietly in her own room, but when she saw these two expectant faces, she rose at once and came. Surely Aurelia had a gift for quick surprise. Now her face flushed; her breath came quick.

"Lavinia, I did not know the tablinium could be so beautiful. And the altar—all in place with flowers and lights. Oh, this is home. We will perform our sacrifice. Then you must tell me about these strange new gods."

As they laid the cakes on the altar and in silence poured the wine upon the pavement in front of it, there was a swift light step and in came Buvinda, uninvited, unannounced. She walked gingerly around the edges of the Orpheus picture, knelt at the altar, and laid primroses and violets upon it. Then she left as quietly as she had come. They did not dare to reprove her, for who could know what god had prompted her act?

CHAPTER EIGHTEEN

NOW, day by day, was the new home established in Britain—a home with those multitudinous interests and industries of which machines have robbed it. And so robbing they have destroyed a precious thing in the world. This home was self-sufficient—or almost so. It afforded occupation and creative work for everybody in it, from the master to the lowest slave. Marcus found himself directing Trogus, or perhaps taking advice from him, as to the cleaning and rebuilding of the stables. The three cows which Favonius had purchased from Vilbia must be better and cleanlier housed. And it was found that Buvinda and Gorm could milk them. All this building and caring for living creatures must go forward under the care of Marcus. The garden was already flourishing, with vegetables on one side of the path and flowers on the other. The old gardener, instead of being a burden, was the most creative worker in the household. Marcus could but catch some of his joy when a new rosebush bloomed or when primroses made a yellow carpet in the garden corner. Here they set the couch for Aurelia, and here the three would gather for their early-evening meal, listening to the nightingales and wondering how these could be here in Britain as well as in far-off Italy.

Lavinia's duties sent her hurrying from the carding-and-spinning room to the spring house and shed for making cheese.

Between these busy hours, she and Marcus went out for a gallop on Triga and Ventus. To the north of the city was a road called the White Road. This led to villas and farms, and here the two would meet other parties of young folk on horseback. Formal greetings led to acquaintance and acquaintance to friendship. The parents came to see Aurelia at "Little Palatine," as Aurelia called their home.

It was the middle of July. They were sitting at their evening meal in the garden when they became aware of some confusion at the gate. They looked and there in the golden light was Favonius, just entering. Aurelia, with a cry, sprang up and ran toward him. Marcus and Lavinia came leaping over the grass to meet him. All three embraced him at one time.

"Oh, Father, Father."

"Oh, Favonius. You are here—here, safe and sound." The garden rang with their happy voices.

The slaves came thronging from all directions, standing first at a little distance, then, when given permission, coming nearer with bows and words of welcome. Favonius held Aurelia at arm's length to look at her.

"Aurelia, you are blooming," he cried. "You don't seem like the same person I left here weeks ago."

Marcus glanced at Lavinia, Lavinia at Marcus. They were safe now from their thrashing.

Next day Favonius had a long talk with Marcus.

"There are uprisings in the north," he told him. "Dangerous

uprisings of the tribes in several quarters. I want you to know but don't tell your mother and Lavinia."

"Oh, they know all about it," answered Marcus. "The neighbors talk of nothing else."

"You are in no danger here. This part of Britannia is fully protected."

"Father, can't I go back with you?" begged Marcus. "Why should I be puttering around the garden like an old woman?"

"And why should I be puttering in Isca," echoed Favonius, "trying delinquent Silurians in the stuffy court rooms, when I ought to be on the fighting line?"

"But can't I go?"

"Not yet, son. I feel safer to have you here. But soon—you shall go. It is your right. At present I have no way of getting you an appointment."

Favonius returned to his post, and swiftly the months went by. October brought nutting parties for the young folk, who went far into the woods, duly protected by their elders. Such gathering of food would have been called slave work in Rome. But here on this frontier of the Empire, life was more natural. Lavinia and Marcus were allowed these simple pleasures that the woods provided. In one of the near-by villas lived a household of young folk, half Roman, half Celt. There were two girls, Fausta and Ageta, and two boys, Flavius and Carminius, both of them taller than Marcus.

Soon it was hardly to be known which home belonged to which family, the young folk were going back and forth so constantly. The Celtic mother in the villa became a good friend for Aurelia.

"Ageta is so pretty," said Lavinia one day as she and Marcus arrived home after a woodland walk.

"Is she?" questioned Marcus. "Yes, I suppose so, but she

seems dull after Neraea. I keep wishing somebody would be as bright and fascinating as Neraea."

"I remember her too," said Lavinia.

"I wrote her a letter last week," confessed Marcus. "Carminius' father was sending a messenger to Nemausis. It was too good a chance to be missed."

Lavinia knew that it meant much for Marcus to write. He to whom writing was as difficult as walking on stilts. Also she knew that he kept the lyre hanging on the wall of his bedroom and the Euripides scroll in a metal box in the corner. These and his sword by the bed were the only things in the room. No, Marcus did not forget. But now he changed the subject.

"Don't you like Carminius?" he asked.

"Yes, I think he sits his horse as beautifully as Father does."

Marcus laughed. "Well, that's a grand way to like a young man."

"Marcus!" Lavinia looked startled—troubled. "Does Mother want me to like Carminius?"

Marcus hesitated. "Well, maybe she does. They're well-bred people and have plenty of fortune."

"Oh, why, why does she think about such things?" Lavinia's hands were trembling now. "Why does she want to get rid of me? I'm perfectly happy here with her."

"Well, Lavinia, you'll have to marry someday. And when Father isn't here, oughtn't Mother to look out for you?"

"No, no," cried Lavinia passionately. "Please, you beg her not to. It was bad enough to marry Decimus."

"Lavinia, you goose—you did not marry Decimus."

"No, but I did almost. Only some god saved me. I'll never forget it. Never, never, never."

By this time Lavinia was crying. And of course Marcus

only laughed at her the more.

"Come, come, sister. Don't be queer. Carminius is a grand fellow. Stop crying and come to supper."

Soon after this began the season when they could see little of their neighbors, Carminius, Ageta, or anybody. Cold rains of November set in, raw as these folk of Italy had never known them. "The days are drawing in," said the folk of Corinium, greeting each other. And indeed the days did draw in, shorter and shorter, as if they were losing breath in this last race of the year. The slaves had to light the lamps at three in the afternoon. And breakfast in the morning was always by lamplight. Lamps of the Romans were a poor defense against darkness. Aurelia was eager to finish a warm cloak for Favonius. She had her loom brought to the tablinium where they burned many lamps, but even so it was difficult to weave save in the middle of the day.

The old slave on the Palatine hill had not been wrong in his statements.

"Well, well"—Aurelia sighed—"at least we are warm. I never was so cosy in Rome." For at the first cold rain, Marcus had had the hypocausts lighted. Great fires of wood in the pits outside. The heat came roaring through flues to the space beneath the floors, up through spaces between walls and out at the queer little chimneys of the roof. The tablinium was warm throughout. The bedrooms above it were warmed and two of the three bathrooms.

"But when we go out it is like a slap in the face," said these folk of sunny Italy.

The rain became sleet. Winds shrieked in the forest. Even when the sun rose, it showed dim through the gray of cloud.

"I'm glad we bought a Nodens," said Marcus as he stood by the altar. "I suppose all this is his doings." But Nodens stood indifferent under the marble canopy.

One morning Lavinia was wakened by Marcus pounding on her door and calling:

"Come out—come out and see the sights."

Even with her one little window glazed with gray glass, Lavinia was aware of a queer white light in the room.

She sprang out of bed, threw on her warmest tunic, belted her toga tight and drew it up short, put on the leather shoes which Britons must wear and her thick cloak. Then she opened her door. She opened it upon a magic world, a world utterly changed. Could that be their wall with its coping of white, its tracery of white lace where the vines clung? Was that rounded mound their holly tree, and who could believe that the long corridor roof could be fringed with something that glittered like a million diamonds?

"Well," laughed Marcus, "don't stand there with your mouth open. Outside on the hills it's twice as fine as the garden. But first put on your woolen buskins; you can't plow through this with bare legs."

Soon they were hurrying out of the gate. Here opened upon their sight a white, white world; no sunlit cloud could be whiter—all creation fresh as on its first morning, the whole landscape breathless as if waiting for some god to pass by. Their familiar meadow dipped down to the vale, its whiteness unsullied by any touch. Long blue shadows led down, down to the silent brook.

Over all arched the sky like an inverted bowl of glass sparkling—not quite friendly; and they breathed an air fragrant with the smell of frost.

"Oh, let's go to the wood," whispered Lavinia.

They hurried, they knew not why. They seemed afraid that all this would disappear. They had seen snow before. Yes, they had seen snow. Warm driblets coming down to melt in the gutters of Rome, or slush made dirty by a hundred passing feet. This snow was another creature.

As they approached the wood, the trees stood like a sparkling phalanx. When they entered, the shadow was an eerie whiteness. The trees were weighted with snow; their branches swept the ground. At the disturbance of these passing feet, they bent and cracked.

"And look, look," begged Lavinia. "Where the little foxes have been running and there a rabbit—do you suppose it was a rabbit and all the tiny claw feet of the birds?"

Of course she had never seen the footprints of woodland creatures.

"It seems as if they were telling us all their stories, of how they come and go," she said.

"It will make grand hunting," remarked Marcus.

"Oh, Marcus, how could you hunt them when they can't help showing all their errands?"

Of course these two discovered they could slide down hill, and of course they did it, until Mother sent Clotho after them to bid them come to breakfast. Yet even so they would not stop until they had brought Aurelia out to see the snow. Here to their astonishment they found that Aurelia could slide as well as they, that she, too, could laugh when they all fell down together.

"Why, Mother," said Marcus, "I thought you were too old."

"I thought so too. Dear me, what would your father say?"

Thus did the land of Britain steal away care from those who came to live within her borders.

CHAPTER NINETEEN

URING THE WINTER Favonius could not travel over the snow-piled roads to see his family. He came in the spring. And he came with great news.

"Falco has been removed. The Emperor has appointed Platorius Nepos as governor of Britannia."

Now Platorius Nepos was a friend of Favonius. They had gone to Spain together at their first entrance into the Roman army. He was a friend of years' standing.

"It may mean much to me," Favonius told them. "It may mean everything."

He stayed only two days in Corinium and hurried on to Londinium to meet the new governor. After a week he returned, a new man, walking more swiftly, talking and laughing more. Platorius had already appointed him tribune in the second legion at Isca. "And he hopes soon to make me *legatus legiones* of the Second Legion Augusta."

This had been a lifelong ambition of Favonius, to be *legatus* of a legion.

At dinner Favonius related the whole interview with the governor.

"Platorius is quite unspoiled," he told them, "in spite of the attentions of the Emperor. He was delighted to find me here in Britain. Says he needs me. 'Remember when your strategy saved a whole cohort in Asturias,' he said. Think of his remembering that! And as I was coming away he said: 'Waste a man like you in the court room. What folly!' He told me about the Emperor's new plans for Britain."

"The Emperor's—plans?" queried Aurelia. Her husband's altered look troubled her.

"He is strengthening the frontiers in the north. It's surely needed. The uprisings grow more terrible every day."

"Favonius, you are not thinking of uprisings. What has happened?" Favonius' face was now clouded in spite of his best effort.

"Well, to tell the truth, the Emperor is coming to Britain."

"The Emperor!" Lavinia sprang up from her chair. To her the Emperor was associated with all harm and evil. "What will he do, Father? Oh, what will he do?"

"Attend to the Emperor's business, I hope," spoke Favonius. "Platorius reassures me. But still the Emperor has a long memory—a long memory."

"I thought we were so far away. I thought he couldn't reach here at all," Lavinia complained.

"He reaches everywhere. Nothing escapes him. He's a veritable storm of energy."

The table, so merry with hopeful talk, grew silent, as if indeed a storm cloud were darkening the horizon.

Aurelia spoke first. "We must depend on Platorius Nepos. If he needs you he'll protect you. There are other men, of course, but not here in Britain—and not men whom Platorius knows and trusts. He's turning to you now, Favonius, to help him in his new office. Let us hope something will happen to make him need you badly."

Marcus hardly heard this talk. He was fidgeting on his couch. He was naturally unafraid of anything. Why should the Emperor want to hurt his father? Father was doing his duty here in Britain. But truth to tell, he was not thinking of Favonius at all.

"Father," Marcus' voice suddenly spoke up, "won't you ask Platorius to do something for me?"

Favonius changed. He even laughed. "Aha, Marcus, I knew you'd be at it. Do something for you? Is that what you want?"

"Yes, Father—can't you ask the governor?"

"No, Marcus. You are too late. I've already asked him. I wasn't going to tell you till tomorrow. But you are at this present moment a centurion in the Second Augusta. So! young man."

Marcus bounded from his couch and stood trembling by his father.

"Father, you are not joking—not joking?"

"No, no, son, how could I joke in so serious a matter? You will go with me in the morning."

But as Marcus stood there, speechless with joy, Lavinia bent low over her plate so that none should see how fast her tears were falling. Marcus was going. She had long dreaded it. Now only separation lay ahead.

Chapter Twenty

NEXT MORNING Marcus did indeed ride away with his father. He was so full of the journey, so proud of the new saddle, the old helmet of his father's, and his own unused sword, that he had no thought at all for Lavinia or her regrets.

"We might meet bandits on the road," he told her in confidence.

"Father never has," said Lavinia.

"Yes, but it's wild country and the Salures are wild—we might! And, anyway, I'll be in camp. By Pollux, I'll be in camp by day after tomorrow."

So he sprang upon Ventus' back, calling to Trogus who was to go with him as body servant.

"Don't cry, young mistress," whispered Trogus.

Lavinia was not crying, but it was a hard battle to keep smiling as she stood by the open gate. She felt sure that never again would she have the happy companionship with Marcus.

And so it proved. During the summer Favonius came home several times. But Marcus, as an inferior officer, had no such privilege. It was in vain she occupied herself in the house, in vain she visited Ageta and Fausta at their villa. She was lonely. Nobody took the place of Marcus.

Often she rode out through the woods with her two girl companions and Carminius, the trusted Clotho always with them. Corinium was surrounded by most beautiful hills, some of them wooded, others bare and rocky. Here blew the salt winds from the sea—so cool on hot days. Carminius called them "hot days," though to the still Roman Lavinia, the days seemed utterly refreshing.

"By Jupiter, isn't it sultry?" remarked Carminius. "Let's eat our lunch on the hilltop."

So up the hill they cantered, and slaves spread a noon-day lunch for them on a flat rock. But the British slaves of Carminius served them with black looks.

"Whatever is the matter?" questioned Lavinia.

Carminius laughed. "Oh, nothing, but that they are afraid. You see this circle of enormous stones." (They were sitting in the midst of the circle.) "Well, the boys are afraid of 'em. Afraid as of Pluto himself."

"Why?" she asked. She and Carminius always had much to talk about. And constantly Aurelia encouraged their being together.

"Well, these Standing Stones are where the old duffers worshiped. Ages and ages ago, and all the forest people here about say the stones are haunted, I believe. Blattus over there would let me kill him rather than send him up here at midnight."

Lavinia's eyes opened wide with that childish wonder which Carminius found so pretty in her. There was fear, too, in her eyes.

"Spirits—evil spirits," he whispered dramatically. "I

wouldn't come up here of nights myself. No, I wouldn't. These stones belonged to the Druids. And the Druids offered human sacrifice to their gods. Oh, not just one person. Hundreds and hundreds. Prisoners of war. They always kept their prisoners alive for the purpose. Wouldn't be surprised if this very flat stone where our lunch is outspread was their altar—spilling blood all down the sides of it."

"Carminius, shame on you," broke in Ageta. "You are just trying to scare Lavinia. You know well Agricola killed all the Druids a hundred years ago."

Carminius wagged his head wisely. "All right, sister, have it your own way. For my part, I don't think we know what these forests hide. Maybe these forests hereabout are cleared. But the forests to the west—why, they're unbroken for fifty miles at a stretch. All sorts of folk hide in 'em. And the Druids, too, I'm thinking."

"Oh, Carminius, you don't really believe that?" remonstrated Lavinia, gazing fixedly at him, forgetting her lunch. "Haven't the Romans conquered Britain? Oh, long ago they did."

"Conquered and yet not conquered. It's easy enough to kill a lot of barbarians. But not so easy to kill their gods. The forest in the west hides both gods and men. Believe me."

"Oh, stop, Carminius," commanded Ageta. "You are spoiling Lavinia's luncheon. See, she eats nothing."

"Lavinia, you dear girl, forget all about it. You're safe here," spoke Carminius, and he poured a full glass of milk for her and gave her a cake from the central platter. He edged nearer to her. "Anyway, I won't let them hurt you."

Lavinia laughed. She knew he was teasing her. And what girl does not love to be teased? Sometimes in these lovely open-air days Lavinia was happy again.

One day in September Lavinia was directing old Vilbas in the garden. There were still flowers, and with care they could keep them going for weeks longer.

"I knows what the flowers wants," chuckled Vilbas. "There's little green creatures lives among 'em. They won't usually come out of the woods, but they stays in my flowers because I speak to 'em soft-like, and 'most every night I puts out porridge for 'em."

"Vilbas, hurry on with your work," commanded Lavinia. But she really knew that nothing ever hurried Vilbas and nothing delayed him either. She bent over a wild rose, tying it up to a little prop. Suddenly Vilbas screamed as one seeing a portent. Lavinia had not noticed the footsteps on the path. She turned and there, glittering in the golden sunshine, stood a centurion, full panoplied. His bronze helm had its tuft of high-spread feathers; on his breast was a phalera or medal—only one for he was young. His shoulders had metal fringes, and of metal bands was his skirt. On one side hung his short sword or gladius, on the other a long sword. Oh, no portent was he to Lavinia! In an instant her arms were close about the bronze-clad shoulders and she was crying, "Marcus, Marcus, Marcus, I thought I'd never see you again."

Marcus gave her a swift smack meant for a kiss.

"I wore all of it," he said shamefacedly, "because I wanted you to see how I look in battle. But there's still the shield."

Indeed, here came Trogus lifting with difficulty the tall shield.

"Oh, Marcus, how strong you look!" Lavinia wanted to say how handsome but did not dare. He was tanned a dark brown, and a rosy glow shone through the tan.

"Have to be strong to stand the discipline. By Pollux, they're rough on a centurion. I've got news for you, sister. I'm fourth centurion in the Ninth now. I'm going north to the Wall."

"But why did they change you?"

"Promotion—promotion. I'm with the vexillation—the picked men of the legion. I'm going now to the fighting line."

"Oh, Marcus, I wish you weren't!"

"Silly. Where's Mother?"

Surely, surely—Mother must not be deprived of this joy for even a moment. They started almost at a run across the garden into the open front door and the tablinium. There sat Aurelia at her spinning. She frankly wept with joy as what Roman mother would not, seeing a beautiful son, full armed, coming into the room. She made no outcry at his going to the fighting line. Was she not long used to that with her husband?

"And I've got news of Father too," Marcus told her. "I saved it for you, Mother. He's *legatus legionis* of the Second Augusta. Mother, your husband commands a legion."

Favonius' dearest ambition! Six thousand men were a legion, and to command them was the highest honor in the army.

"Oh, Marcus, Marcus," was all Aurelia could say, and she said that falteringly. To have her loved one win his prize while still in the fullness of powers! It took her breath away with joy.

"You see, the old general of the Second died," Marcus rattled on. "He was terribly old—almost fifty—so it was about time he gave up. And the minute Platorius heard it he made the new appointment to Father. So the Emperor will confirm it when he comes. Now if only there'll be some strong uprisings in Caledonia so Father will have to go, it will please His Imperial Majesty and then—"

The slaves were venturing in with evening meal. All had

some respectful greeting for Marcus. And all showed joyous faces. For they were proud of this young master.

"Come, dear boy"—Aurelia put her arm about his shoulder—"take off the heavy armor and have some old-fashioned home-cooked food. It will taste good after the army mess."

"Indeed, indeed it will." And Marcus' ready laugh rang through the house.

The whole visit was passed for Lavinia in a flash of joy. So quickly over, so quickly spent. And yet in all their hours together she was constantly aware of a change in Marcus. The gallops in the wood, the meeting with the neighboring young folk all secondary now. His thought was with the army. A kind of condescension was in his manner, a swagger of pride. He was rough with the slaves.

"So," thought Lavinia, "must he treat the soldiers of his century."

At the end of the three days he was eager to be gone. And Lavinia well knew that before a mile was traced he would have forgotten her and Mother, thinking only of the duties ahead.

A few weeks later came Favonius on a flying visit. Anyway, Father was not changed. What the army could do to him it had done long ago. But he was stronger, a sense of attainment about him. A sense of establishment in Britain. . .

"Aurelia," he said one day as they walked about the garden and the stables and the grove beyond the wall, "do you still regret Rome?"

"How strange of you to ask. I was thinking myself this morning that I do not. Lavinia and Marcus are so happy here. You have got your rights at last. Of course, I often long for Mother and my sisters, but not for Rome. Yes, we are Britons now."

Favonius, too, had news. His legion, the Second, at least a part of it was ordered north with Favonius in command to quell a rising near Eboricum. So at the coming of the Emperor he would be busy and needed. Their fear of the Emperor was almost gone.

And now all Britain was given over to one thought, one expectancy. "The Emperor is coming! The Emperor is coming!" "Will October stay bright?" "Will the fall rains keep off until after the amazing visit?" "He is traveling from Germany." "He will land at Dubris." "No, he will land at Londinium." "Has not Londinium ordered to be made a colossal statue to welcome the divine one!"

In every town and city the Emperor worship was revived by the priests who had that in charge, and had (if the truth be told) been neglecting it. This one religion close to the Roman heart was not so close to the heart of Britain. And this man—this Hadrian—was not a Roman, not even an Italian. He was born of unroyal parents in Spain. Yet he had the right of life and death over the millions of subjects of the Roman Empire. At this time—the fifth year of his reign—he was not the pathetic object which later he was to become. He was strong—tireless—constructive.

At last the human god arrived, and the farthest savage living in his dugout in the north or in the western mountains heard news of that arrival. Without rest or respite he went from city to city, from district to district, traveling magnificently upon his horse, hailed and worshiped—the picture of an Emperor. But when he got to work, he dismounted from his horse, went afoot into the region he intended to change. His friends in Rome called it "Hadrian's British walking tour."

He had great plans for Britain and soon all Britain was buying with those plans.

"The Wall—The Wall." That word was on every lip; that enterprise stirred every city and every Roman legion. Men were arriving from Gaul, from Germany, from Hispania, to work upon the Wall—centuries and cohorts from every legion were detailed to march north and work upon the Wall. The governor, Platorius Nepos, was in charge of the construction. Plans were drafted and abandoned. Plans were remade and put to effect. It was to be the biggest frontier work in the whole Roman Empire—even more imposing than the frontiers of Germany.

Indeed, if Britain was to be held by the Romans, the Wall was needed. Never for long were the northern tribes placated. Terrific rebellions were now breaking out all along the north. The South of Britain was safe but only at the price of almost constant fighting. The Romans had taken Britain by the sword and they must hold it by the sword. Yes, the Wall was needed.

This Wall of Hadrian's was to be seventy-five miles long, stretching from shore to shore across the island. Over rocky heights, across rivers, across fields and fens would it go. It would be twenty feet high including the parapet. It would be eight feet thick at the base. At every mile would be a fort as part of the Wall—a mile-castle—and these would be garrisoned. Between these were towers where sentries would watch. In front, that is, to the north of the Wall, was to be a ditch or fosse nine feet deep and thirty-four feet across. This would run all the seventy-five miles. Prodigious work. With what wonder did the blue-painted Picts and the Caledonians view such industry. Such tons of earth removed, such tons of stone piled up. Such days and months and years at the work.

Hadrian traveled over the whole island and departed, leaving Platorius Nepos in charge of building the Wall.

Before he left he confirmed the Platorius appointment of Favonius Claudius as legate of the Second Augusta.

Chapter Twenty-One

GAIN Aurelia and Lavinia faced the long British winter, and faced it alone. Neither Favonius nor Marcus came south during those dark and stormy months. The building of the Wall could not go forward in the winter snow, but constant guard was needed against the restless Caledonians and Picts. It seemed as though these barbarians feared the Wall and wanted to make a last fight before it was set up. Three letters during these long hard months came from Favonius by special messenger. With one of these was a letter from Marcus, short and so inexpressive that Marcus might be suspended in space for all it told of him.

"At least he is alive. At least he is well," said Lavinia ruefully when she read the letter aloud.

"I hope his father keeps in touch with him," sighed Aurelia. "But I am sure Marcus is doing his duty."

At last came spring. Oh, welcome as no southern spring can be, welcome and green and living. And in this spring Lavinia was sixteen years old.

To most young girls and boys at the age of sixteen there

comes an unearthly beauty. It has little to do with features or previous appearance. It is as if at this time the gods set their seal upon their work and say, "Here is perfection; here is the zenith." This beauty lasts about six months or at most a year and then is gone, never to return. Afterward the young person may be handsome, noticeable, compelling. But that ethereal look like an appearance of divinity is not there again. And now this look settled upon Lavinia. So young, so full of grace, she seemed the embodiment of the spring.

In her childhood Lavinia had resembled her paternal grandmother—a severe Roman woman. Now Lavinia quite suddenly looked like her mother, and without question, Aurelia was beautiful.

But Lavinia was discontented. She was tired of Carminius and wanted to get away from his neighborhood, but knew not where to go. There was something she was always wishing for, but she did not quite know what it was. She would answer her mother harshly and then wonder why Aurelia did not reprove her. And she was certainly rude to Carminius.

Carminius would flush hotly. "Look here, Lavinia *mea*, I won't be spoken to that way. I'm through with you."

Then he would gallop away on his horse, leaving Lavinia to ride home with his sisters.

She liked Carminius better when he was angry with her. But she did not like him to make love to her as he was frankly doing now. He knew that both Aurelia and Favonius approved of him.

And now again the thought of Decimus tortured her. He seemed to stand at the door of her thoughts with drawn sword against all love or happiness. Must she go through with such another day as her wedding day in Rome—the long night vigil, the guests arriving at dawn? Would not Carminius at the last moment call her ugly? As for her present good looks, they were not of the sort to be observed in a dull metal mirror. Long study of her mirror told Lavinia nothing.

When at last Favonius returned it was of Lavinia that he spoke first of all.

"She's grown up," he told his wife as they sat together in the garden. "She's fully grown and it's high time she was married. Soon she will be too old."

"Oh, Favonius!"

"Yes, she will. What girl is married beyond sixteen, or at most seventeen? Marriages at nineteen are half a disgrace."

"Nevertheless, she seems so young."

Favonius did not listen.

"I'm ashamed of her the way she acts about young Carminius. There's no better young man in Britain. His father has a good position in the army; they have money and live near by. And I really think the lad is fond of her."

"Yes, but is she fond of him?"

"There you are—there you are," said Favonius wrathfully. "This foolish freedom of the British frontier! I tell you, Aurelia, it's all wrong, the young folk seeing each other and taking fancies. We'll have her married now while I am here. Before a week she will be perfectly contented. I don't see why you pay such heed to her disobedient ways."

"Wait, Favonius, please wait."

"No, I won't wait. I shall speak to Carminius' father today and complete the betrothal. When Lavinia knows she has to marry there'll be no words about it."

Nothing more was to be said when Favonius spoke in that tone. Yet Aurelia had a deep instinct that Lavinia would not be contented. "Oh," she thought, "I wish I could find out what ails this daughter of mine. We may do much harm by this haste."

Meanwhile Lavinia was all too aware that her father was urging the marriage. She saw it in his sharp glances at her when she entered the tablinium, in her mother's troubled face at table. What were they deciding? What should she do? If there were only a place somewhere to which she could run and hide. The woods, the hills, or one of those hut towns of the Britons. Was there any spot where they could not find her? If she could only get away until Father was gone. Mother, by herself, would be kinder. Yet she avoided Aurelia too. All day she saw to it that she was never alone with her—never a chance to talk.

But that night after she was in bed came Aurelia into the room. Lavinia sat up, clasping and unclasping her hands. Her heart was pounding so she could scarcely speak. Aurelia was looking at her so solemnly.

"Mother, Mother, don't speak to me! Please don't tell me!"

Aurelia set down the lamp she was carrying and took both Lavinia's trembling hands in her own. She spoke caressingly.

"Daughter—what is the matter? Try to tell me."

"Oh, I don't want to marry again. I don't want another day like my wedding day."

"My darling, what nonsense! You have never been married."

"It's Decimus. Always Decimus. He said I was ugly. Nobody loves an ugly girl. He ran away."

Lavinia's voice was high pitched and wild. She began to sob. Aurelia sat down on the couch, smoothing Lavinia's hands.

"But, Lavinia, Decimus is not here. Decimus is gone—gone out of your life."

A light broke over Aurelia. Her child was haunted by that dreadful young man! What should she do to break the spell?

It was the evil eye.

"Lavinia, listen. Stop crying; listen. Don't you know there are a hundred chances that Decimus is dead. In battle, by disease! Oh, a hundred chances. His ghost cannot follow you. I won't let it. I'll sacrifice to Juno against him. He shan't touch you."

Lavinia clung to her mother.

"Remember, dear, Carminius is not like Decimus. He loves you. He is a kind and good young man. You would always be near me, and Carminius has been good to me, too, like a son. You cannot fail to love a man as good as Carminius. Even when you have been sharp with him, he has been kind."

Lavinia's sobs began to grow quiet.

"You'll sacrifice against Decimus, Mother? You know the right thing to do?"

"Yes, yes, dear, I know." Aurelia was not sure but she would not tell this to Lavinia. She rose with decision.

"Now, daughter, wait a moment while I go and consult Father. I will come back."

Aurelia had courage now for she had something to tell her husband.

"Well, well," said Favonius impatiently when he had heard her out. "I don't believe in charms myself, but if you and Lavinia do, well and good. I saw Carminius' father this afternoon and he is glad of the alliance. But he does not want the betrothal until after his older son is married. We are to complete it when I come next time. Meanwhile, I want you and Lavinia to make a visit to Aqua Sulis. You have both been housed up too long. The crowds and the new sights there will help you. And the waters are wonderful. Charms and love potions indeed! I'm ashamed of you, Aurelia."

Aurelia kissed him gratefully.

"You always know best," she said. And she meant it. Even she knew that a little absence from Carminius would exorcise his rival's ghost better than any charm.

She returned to Lavinia, her face bright with the good news.

"Only think, we shall go to Aqua Sulis." Then she sat by Lavinia's bed holding her hand until she went to sleep.

"What a child she is," thought Aurelia, "in spite of her sixteen years."

CHAPTER TWENTY-TWO

EXT DAY Favonius rode away northward. The division of his legion remaining in Isca Salures would require him back again in a few weeks—so Aurelia was happy in the thought of his quick return.

Then how strange it was the very next day to have the old *raeda* brought out, its curtains washed, its cushions renewed. What memories it brought of the miles upon miles of travel! And now they were to travel again. At first Lavinia was indifferent. The marriage which she knew now was so certain weighed upon her. But once upon the road, the horses plodding southward, the scene constantly changing, she herself was unperceptibly changed. Clotho, of course, was with them, and Stephana, Lavinia's maid, the hostler, also two mounted slaves who were to act as messengers. Many roads converged at Corinium. Of these they took the Fosse Way, leading southwestward—a good road and much traveled by the invalids who were continually visiting the healing waters.

They arrived at Aqua Sulis at nightfall, found good rooms, and retired. They did not see the famous place until next morning. The Roman town of Bath had none of the quaint beauty it was to acquire after centuries of habitation. It was new, blatantly new and highly ornamental, with temples and Corinthian colonnades, with open squares and a handsome basilica. On every building were reliefs, sculptures, goddesses, nymphs, cupids, leaves and flowers. Lavinia was much astonished.

"Oh, Mother, it's like Rome," she said.

"No, daughter, it is not like Rome. These are not great statues such as Rome has gotten from Athens and Corinth. It is not even fine Roman work."

Lavinia could not see the difference.

"It isn't as big," she said, at which her mother laughed.

They came to the temple of Sulis, the local goddess of the city. Its pediment was graced with a large and terrible face, a mask with snakes instead of hair, a frown of horror contracting the forehead.

"Oh, whatever is that?" queried Lavinia. "He looks as if he is in pain."

"Perhaps it is one of the patients. Perhaps he is put there to scare away evil spirits," guessed Aurelia.

"He'd surely scare away me," thought Lavinia, but of course she did not speak aloud such an impious thought.

The baths were large and luxurious, even the part reserved for women. Here in the great pools the water came gushing from the earth boiling hot, filling the apartment with blinding steam and smelling of the strange substances which were supposed to cure pain. The place was crowded with patients. It did not occur to these Romans to question why the water came boiling and steaming from the depth, or why its medicines had decided properties. The Roman mind lacked the spirit of wonder which kept the Greek mind so alert and young. Even Aurelia and her daughter went through the large and lofty apartments, taking the various baths with no such curiosity. But Lavinia was interested in the new people, the new faces. The patients were from everywhere, northern Gaul, southern Gaul, and the foreign region of Germany, and of course from every quarter of Britain. During the day she forgot about her coming marriage; only at night did she have to push the thought from her.

"I will not be far from home," she kept telling herself. "Carminius surely will let me see Mother every day. And I can show Vilbas what to do with the flowers, and Clotho about the spinning."

By day they met the many strangers. She heard about rich lands and cities and great rivers in far-away Germany. But after a week she grew tired even of this.

"They are all so old, Mother," she complained as they rested after the bath by the great forty-foot pool. "There's not one young girl like me."

"Well, daughter, young people are fortunately healthy. They don't have to come to Aqua Sulis to be cured."

"And, oh, Mother, they are all so sick and pale and funny looking, and why can't they talk of something beside their diseases? Talk, talk, talk all day long about horrid things that happen to their bodies. I begin to feel my bones ache too."

"Lavinia," said her mother sadly, "you are hard to please. You used to be so contented."

Their talk was interrupted by an outcry that was almost a screech, and from the farthest edge of the pool came a stout woman running, dragging her bath robe, calling, "Aurelia— Aurelia Claudia."

At first Aurelia's face went blank; then suddenly she ran to meet the woman with outstretched arms.

"Marcia—Marcia—how can you be here, Marcia?"

"Oh, Aurelia—I knew you lived in Britannia. But didn't know where. I tried and tried to find you."

They tripped over each other's words in eagerness to explain, Marcia talking so loud that everybody was looking. They forgot Lavinia. But Lavinia, standing there, did well remember this woman in Rome. She used often to come to see them on the Clivus Victoriae.

"And this is my daughter," said Aurelia, at last drawing Lavinia forward.

"So tall! Why, she's a woman grown. And surely she didn't use to be so pretty and healthy looking. I wish I had a daughter, so I do. But my boys are fine."

"And how is Philippa?" queried Aurelia.

"Oh, but Philippa is here in Britannia," declared Marcia. "She didn't come with me to Aqua. She's out at my home in Dumnores. She's just come to visit—just arrived and too tired she was to come here with me."

This Philippa was Marcia's sister, and though Aurelia had always known Marcia, she loved Philippa who had been her dearest friend in Rome.

"Oh, I wish I could see her," said Aurelia as eagerly as a girl.

"Philippa saw your mother in Rome the very last thing before she left," so Marcia went on. "Your mother looks so old and broken. Philippa brought messages from her."

"Oh dear, oh dear," spoke Aurelia still more wistfully.

"How long have you been here at Aqua Sulis?" questioned Marcia.

"Oh, we've barely come. We'll be here quite a while."

"But I won't. My visit ends tomorrow. What a shame! So much to tell you."

Suddenly Marcia had an idea, and with one of her little screams (how familiar were those to Aurelia) she seized her friend's arm.

"I've got it. You come home with me tomorrow. Visit me instead of the baths. You can see Philippa and everything."

"But I couldn't go without asking my husband," said Aurelia.

"Where is he?"

"Far north on the frontier."

"Foolish. Of course you can come. You can send word home and leave word here. Surely Favonius is not so strict as that."

Lavinia added her pleading. How wonderful to see the west country, wild and strange.

"And I'd love to hear about Grandmother," urged Lavinia, "and maybe Philippa saw Aemilia, too, and Aunt Rhoda."

Before long Aurelia had consented. She dispatched one of her messengers to Corinium telling of her decision and kept the other slaves for the journey. Next morning the familiar *raeda* was again brought forth, Marcia's *cisium* and slaves beside it.

Thus all unexpectedly, as so often happens with our best adventure, the travelers found themselves going to a land and life unknown. They again took the Fosse Way—at first southwest, then straight for the sea.

"Marcia," said Aurelia anxiously on the second day, "I had no idea the way was so far."

Marcia laughed easily. "We're almost halfway now," she said.

To Lavinia the way could not be too long. This road winding ever into wilder and wilder country, this unbroken forest with its unearthly silence which almost frightened her.

They went forward into the full tide of spring, that spring of the north, swift with a sort of ecstasy. It was as if all the pent-up longings and refusals of the winter had suddenly broken into freedom—into the full consent of earth and sky.

The leaves of the trees were not quite open, shining with a verdancy more gold than green. The forest roof was thin, filtering in the light. Small wood flowers, taking their chance before the density of shade, bloomed in great sheets of color. That purple stretch was the homeland of violets. That white was "snowdrops." In the gashes of the hillsides ran the wild thyme, smelling, as one of the poets of this land has said, "like dawn in Paradise." Flowers were here that were to sing in poetry for centuries to come, flowers which were to disappear forever beneath the foot of men. The very land itself "dreamed and dwelt apart."

Some lands depend upon the coming of man to give them character. They must wait until human beings make history. Other lands are character in themselves and impose that character upon all comers.

It was into such a land that Lavinia was now entering. As yet no knight rode forth to rescue the afflicted, no king held council at a table round, no castle frowned upon the heights. Yet the spirit of all this was there to be felt at once. And whosoever came must act as this land pleased. This land was remote, and through all its history remote it would remain. It thrust itself out from Britain into the western sea and it breathed into itself the mystery and terror of the sea. Far at its western end was a cape almost unknown to men—a region someday to be called Lyonesse. Someday this land would prosper. Princes would live there; saints would walk there; bells would ring from stone towers calling men to a worship yet unborn. Then in one dark and terrible night the sea would rise and claim Lyonesse for its own. Down, down it would sink to be seen no more.

It would become the Lost Land there on the ocean floor. But ghostly bells would ring beneath the waves; mermaids would wait dangerously on rocks awash, and the lonely fisherman leaning over his gunwale could see the streets of silent cities. Ay, this land knows that men are her children, to be taught of her, and when she wills she destroys them.

At night the travelers camped by the roadside for there were no towns. Lavinia was blissful in this open beauty. They awoke in dewy freshness with larks singing, invisible in the blue. Now the road twisted and plunged down into steep valleys, between bare, rocky hills. Now in the silence they heard the distant roar of the sea. A mist came stealing in from seaward. Dark clouds gathered overhead, and a soft rain began.

Suddenly in the quiet of their going they heard a sound like the distant quacking of ducks. Nearer, nearer it came. No, it was like the howl of a wolf pack. The slaves hurried their horses. The women had not yet taken fright. Now came the gallop of hoofs closer, closer like the onslaught of a storm.

Then all happened so quickly that one hardly drew breath before the thing was done.

A dozen horsemen appeared in the ravine, yellow hair flying, red scarfs tossing in their swift flight, yelling their barbarous war cry.

"The Durotrigs!" screamed Marcia. But no one heard her.

The troop dashed down upon the party, scattering them right and left. They overturned the *raeda,* and the horses broke loose and galloped up the road. They stabbed Aurelia's hostler as he tried to protect her, took her other slaves prisoners. As for Marcia's slaves, they one and all fled, screaming away like frightened birds.

Lavinia was aware of all this through a close mist of horror. She knew that the *raeda* went over in darkness. That the struggling horses screamed like human beings. She knew that evil-smelling men were dragging her out, were dragging her mother from the ruins. She knew she was fighting the men to save herself, and that Mother was saying,

"Keep still, daughter, it's the only way."

She knew that Marcia was screaming almost as loudly as the horses and that the retreating gallop of the *raeda* team seemed the last sound she was ever to hear on earth.

Then she and Mother were tied together with ropes. They were walking along the highway between men who seemed more like beasts than men. Marcia could hardly walk and they prodded her along with their spears. Lavinia heard Mother give a gasping sob as they were turned off the highway into the hills and the last door of their hope was closed. It was a rough narrow path which the Durotrigs seemed to know, and it led away from the sea into the wilderness. Mother was holding her hand very tight.

"Daughter," came her low voice, "if we come to a stream, I will squeeze your hand suddenly; then we will throw ourselves into the water. Drowning is best."

"Yes, Mother," said Lavinia steadily.

She was going to die. She, Lavinia. All the beauty of life, over and done. No day nor night any more. She was going to die. Mother was going to die. What would Father do? And what would Marcus do when he heard his sister was gone? Marcus would care about it. Yes, yes, up there in the north he would feel horrified and lost.

How silly she had been to be cross with Mother because she missed Marcus. She'd try not to. Oh, gods, there was no more chance to try. Many Roman women had killed themselves at times like this. These were Roman heroines. But Lavinia did not feel heroic. She only felt she was going to die and did not want to. Oh, gods, she must not think about it. Oh, now—now they had come to a stream!

All streams had to be forded. Thank heaven this one was deep. Yes, deep enough! They waded into the ford and were soon up to their knees. Oh—oh—Mother was squeezing her hand hard. Could they do it? Could they—

Now Aurelia jerked Lavinia forward and to the left where the water looked swift and swirling. The men had not kept hold. They thought the water was enough to hold their prisoners. Together Aurelia and Lavinia leaped. Instantly, tied as they were, they sank. Cold and strangling, the water closed over their heads.

"Yes, yes, it will kill us," raced Lavinia's thoughts. "It is killing us now, now, now."

But the two keepers were not to be deprived of their prizes. With yells and Celtic curses they leaped in after them. The center current of the stream was deep and swift but narrow, and the men soon had their victims dragged up to the rocks, then to the shore itself.

"Oh, we didn't do it. We didn't do it," wailed Lavinia. But her whole being rejoiced that she was not dead. Drenched with streaming garments, shaking, chattering with cold—but "not dead, not dead," sang Lavinia's heart.

Aurelia swayed and sank to the ground, dragging Lavinia with her.

"Oh, Mother, Mother, don't die," sobbed Lavinia. "Don't die and leave me."

And at Lavinia's call, Aurelia's eyes opened; color came back to her face—at least a little. As for their keepers, curiously enough they were not angry. They laughed loudly. The others crowded round, evidently making fun of the keepers. They nodded at each other. It was plain to see they admired the two women for their act. One of the young men took off his red-striped cloak and wrapped it around Lavinia, then lifted both her and Aurelia to their feet. The coat smelled like old fish but Lavinia was thankful to have it, thankful when another man similarly wrapped her mother.

And now exhausted and colder than they had ever been in their lives, Lavinia and her mother plodded on with the others. Up, up a steep hill, then down on the other side into the wood again. The rain drizzled, wetting the cloaks, but their misery was beyond knowing it. Lavinia had lost control and was sobbing softly, insistently. All Aurelia's assurances and reproofs seemed to do no good.

Marcia kept offering the men reward if they would free them, forgetting that they did not understand, perhaps wisely knowing they *would* understand money in any language.

They began to hear the cracking of twigs, the whinnying of a horse.

Lavinia was too stunned to notice it. But the warriors stopped, looking warily into the forest.

"Daughter," warned Aurelia, "we are coming to their settlement. Don't give up—we'll manage somehow. We'll manage."

Lavinia knew what Mother meant.

Then all of a sudden, incredibly, horribly, they were in the midst of another pitched battle.

CHAPTER TWENTY-THREE

HE ATTACKING WARRIORS broke out from the thicket and fell upon the Durotrigs with yells of terrifying vigor. Instantly swords were clashing right above the heads of Lavinia and Aurelia. Arms flashed in front of their faces and the swords scraped against each other, fending and thrusting. The man next to Lavinia let go his hold. He was stabbed through the neck and fell with a groan. The man beside Aurelia leaped forward and grasped an antagonist with both arms. The horses, hot and sweaty, brushed Lavinia's shoulders. There was no thinking, planning, reasoning. All she could do was to crouch down with her mother and try to avoid the blows. The contestants moved along the path like a boiling tide. The two women found themselves left behind.

"Quick. Into the woods," cried Aurelia. She threw her arm about Lavinia's shoulders so they might move together, tied as they were. They ran into the woods, fell on hidden rocks, struggled up again and pushed on—on. Lavinia kept holding her mother from falling. "I am the stronger. I can save her," she suddenly thought. Ah, here was a huge tree fallen across their way. Lavinia pulled her mother toward the crown of it. But it seemed to branch everywhere, and vines with which it was matted made a complete tangle with the next tree. She turned toward the roots. As to the fallen trunk, they could not possibly climb over that. Now they found the roots unexpectedly large—roof high and thrusting in every direction. These caught them, tore their garments, scratched their faces. As they tried to round the far end of the rootage, they stumbled and fell into the cavelike hollow made by the torn-up roots.

Aurelia pulled her daughter down into a heap.

"Crouch low, crouch low," she commanded. But there was no need of such command. They were already crouching under the cover of the roots.

"We are getting away. We are getting away," Lavinia's mind repeated over and over. "And we are alive, alive."

They could hear the stamping, galloping and screaming of the fight. It was not far off. Indeed it was much too near.

"I wish we could run farther," whispered Lavinia. But there was no use to wish it for the hollow was deep, and the roots crossed and twisted into it. To climb out was impossible.

"We are hidden," answered Aurelia desperately.

Now the noise lessened, diminished off like some cruel thunder. They could hear the gallop and urge of horses. Was that the Durotrigs running away or the attackers?

"Why did the Durotrigs fight each other?" Lavinia found voice to ask.

"It was not from their settlement," said Aurelia. "It was some enemy of theirs."

Now voices were calling, calling in the woods. Men were coming to find the prisoners, thrashing the bushes as they came. There, they must have found Marcia for Marcia screamed. Oh, closer, closer the heavy footsteps. Now the words—they could hear the words. Great heaven, these were Latin words!

"Where are you? Answer, answer."

And then later:

"Don't be afraid! Oh, answer me, answer!"

Such a clear voice, such pleading in it. Lavinia stirred. How foolish, she had almost called out. Aurelia was holding her close, crouching lower. Now the man, whoever he was, had come to the tree.

"No," he was saying to himself. "They could not get past this. Oh, where are they?"

He started off in another direction, hesitated, came slowly back, walking straight for their hiding place. Now he was pushing aside the root. He was peering down upon them. He summoned his followers.

"Lucius, Lucius"—how his voice rang out!—"I've found them. Come and help me."

He leaped into the hollow. Oh, he was a Roman, short haired, clean shaven. He even had on a Roman tunic and corslet.

"Don't be afraid, *domina*. You are safe now. Believe me."

Aurelia suddenly burst into tears, as if her long rigor gave way.

The young man bent over them. "What is the matter?" he was asking, wondering at their helplessness. When he saw they were tied, he made an exclamation of wrath, whipped out his sword, all reeking and bloody as it was, cut the ropes, and lifted them both to their feet. Aurelia could hardly stand, and he put his arm about her, saying nothing but holding her steady. Now Lucius came to the edge of the hollow.

"God in heaven," quoth Lucius. "The poor ladies, like rabbits caught."

"Here, Lucius," said the young man, "take hold of her shoulders." And he lifted Aurelia straight upward as if she were nothing. Then he turned to Lavinia. He did not lift her at once but gazed into her face with some intent inquiry. Whatever his question, it seemed soon answered.

"Now," he said with almost gaiety. "Hold yourself stiff. So—up you go."

And swiftly Lavinia felt herself rise, weightless, to the edge of the pit where Lucius caught her and dragged her to the level. Instantly the young man was there too.

"Help the other woman, Lucius," he commanded, taking Lavinia from the older man's grasp and beginning to guide her back to the path. They were soon there. Oh, what a little way had the two prisoners run in the wood!

Here on the path was all the sad litter of the fight—torn scarves, broken swords, two men dead—one of them the very young man who had given Lavinia his cloak—a third wounded, helpless. The rain came softly down, pattering the leaves overhead. Ah, upon how many battlefields through the centuries has fallen the English rain.

Now along the way came Marcia, supported by one of the Romans. She was weeping loudly, evidently not reassured by these new rescuers. With her were Clotho and Stephana, who throughout the march had been kept in the rear of the party. Marcia was set down next to where Lavinia and Aurelia sat, exhausted, on the earth.

"I know who these people are," she whispered. "They're the folk of a strange religion. They drink the blood of children at their feasts."

"Oh, hush, hush," said Aurelia. "We must take what comes."

Now the young leader was busy everywhere. He seemed to move with an energy which was not spent with the spending.

His men seemed not so much to obey him as to share his purpose. They were a motley troop, some Romans and dressed as Romans, some Celts with long hair and sweeping mustaches, some young, some old.

"Catch the horses," was his first order. "How many are there?"

"We've caught ours already, and there's one of the Durotrigs' ponies."

"Good." The leader hurried forward and bent over the wounded man. Lavinia closed her eyes for she did not want to see him spear the enemy—so as to leave him dead on the field. But the young man did no such thing.

"Oh, he isn't badly off; he'll live. Put him on his own pony. Give me that piece of scarf." He skillfully bound up the man's bleeding leg.

"You see, you see," whispered Marcia, "he's saving him for a human sacrifice."

Fear entered Lavinia again. It came into her mind like a sickness. Must she go back to horror and danger? Would they sacrifice her also and Mother, lay them on top of an altar, knifing them there? It was instantly a picture in her thought and she was too exhausted to push it away.

"Put the fat woman on a horse," the young man ordered next. "Now bring my horse and the donkey."

He did not wait for this last to be obeyed but hurried and brought the beasts himself.

"*Domina*," he said kindly to Aurelia, "we are going to Avalonia, the Island of Glass."

This meant nothing to Aurelia but Marcia cried out, "I don't want to go to Avalonia. I know what it is."

"Nevertheless, madame, you must go there as fast as the horse can trot," he answered her. "The Durotrigs may return."

He put Aurelia on the horse. Then he turned to Lavinia. She was so tired it seemed impossible that she should mount the little donkey. But he lifted her and she sat astride.

"Ah, I see you are a rider," he commented.

She tried to hold the reins but her hands fumbled. He took them from her, then put his hand against her back to support her, and they started forward, he walking beside her. Oh, how good felt his warm strong hand upon her back. She was conscious of nothing else.

"You ought to be with Mother." She suddenly said her thought aloud. "She needs you more than I."

"Lucius is with her," he answered. "He will not let her fall."

"But that wouldn't be you," said Lavinia.

She felt his hand stir as if with pleasure.

"But I shall stay with you all the way," he said as if to a little child.

Now why did she say that silly thing? Her senses did not seem to be working. Whatever she thought she spoke.

On and on they went, following the narrow path underneath the trees. They were among steep, rocky hills. The Black Down Hills, called Black even then. Slowly the dim daylight faded. They made a turn onto a more traveled road.

"This road is our road," he commented. "It is safer."

She was so cold and her garments so wet with the rain that she began to shake and her teeth to chatter.

"Amplias," he called, "I lost my cloak in the fight. Won't you lend me yours?"

"Yes, Govan, of course."

She was dully aware of a big Celt riding near. Then the young man was wrapping her round and round in a thick cloak. Oh, never was a cloak so warm, so woolly-good to feel.

Warmer, warmer with her wet dress steaming inside it.

"His name is Govan." This kept repeating in her mind to the rhythm of the donkey's step. "His name is Govan, Govan."

Now she suddenly heard the click-click of the donkey's hoofs upon the stones and was aware that for a space she had heard nothing. She was sinking forward. She had been asleep. The young man's arm went around her, holding her in the warm cloak, supporting her on the donkey. "Poor child," she heard him say. "Poor little girl."

"I'm grown up," she thought, "and he doesn't know it."

Sleeping, waking, conscious, unconscious, then startled by sudden noise or turn, Lavinia journeyed on through the night. They came down from the hills and traveled in the marsh country, flat and heavy with mist. That night might have been a hundred hours. Lavinia did not know when they began to mount a steep hill. The early spring dawn was beginning to break as they reached the top of the tor.

Then lights flashed through the village hither and yon. People came running.

"What is it? What's happened?"

"It's Govan's men. They've returned."

"Who are the women?"

Such was the confusion of questions all about.

Then Govan's voice:

"The Durotrigs. They'd caught a party of travelers. The women were nearly dead when we found them. Mother, we'll take the lady and her daughter."

Everybody was talking. Everybody helping.

"We'll get food ready."

"Yes, the fire in the big kitchen."

"Yes—yes."

But it was all dim and unreal to Lavinia. She reached for her mother's hand. Yes, Mother was safe. Now they were in a small room somewhere. The warm cloak was being unwrapped by kind and ready hands. This must be the one whom Govan called Mother. Oh, what a warm soft sheepskin on the floor. No, she did not want any food, only sleep, sleep. And Mother was beside her.

Then Lavinia knew nothing more.

Chapter Twenty-Four

LAVINIA AWOKE after an eternity to hear voices. They were talking at the open door. The voices had roused her.

"Son, don't be so impatient. It would be natural if she slept all day."

"Oh, do you think she will?" That was the young man speaking—the young man whose name was Govan.

"But think what she has suffered. Be thankful that she can sleep and be restored." That was his mother.

"But I want her to come. I want her to come right now. The people have waited three hours. They won't wait any longer. I've begged them to wait."

The mother laughed indulgently. "Son, you cannot order everything to your liking. Be patient."

He began to pace up and down, anything but patiently.

"Is her mother awake?"

"Yes, the mother awoke. We have been talking together. Govan, she is a lovely woman."

"Of course she is. Of course. They are both lovely. We want them both."

Lavinia was fully awake now. She rose out of the bed. She

was muscle-sore but rested. But most of all she was puzzled. What in the world did the young man mean? "We want them both. The people won't wait." Like a horrid bolt of lightning flashed the thought in Lavinia's mind—human sacrifice! Marcia's statements! After all, Marcia lived near this place and should know about it. Feasts with children's blood! Oh, what must she do now? She turned a terrified face to her mother.

"Don't be frightened, Lavinia," Aurelia said steadily. "The woman—our hostess—has been wonderfully kind. I like her. There is something about her—"

But here the woman turned toward them in the doorway, speaking to her son.

"They are awake," she told him. "Go tell the people to wait."

She helped Lavinia to dress, brought her warm water and a rough tunic of her own, gave her a comb and bone pins for her hair. It did not occur to the woman to call Lavinia's maid. Aurelia was already dressed.

A high-toned bell began to ring clear and as if with summons.

"We will go now," said their hostess.

They came out into the village, a very un-Roman place with small houses grouped about a central field. But everywhere, in this central green, under the trees, near the houses, were people. Even Aurelia looked startled as she saw them.

"It is the *collecta*," the woman explained. "We celebrate the rising of our Lord."

This meant nothing to Lavinia. But, oh, it was plainly a sacrifice. The people were coming from every direction. They were greeting each other—telling each other some news, upon which others answered as if with the gladness of surprise. As Lavinia and her mother came nearer, they could hear what was said.

"Christ is risen."

And the answer:

"Yea, the Lord is risen indeed."

Even little children lisped the answer.

Oh, that was it. These people were Christians. That was what Marcia meant. And Lavinia knew about Christians. Had not Ino filled her with stories in the nursery? They drank children's blood. That was what Ino said too. They were always interfering with Ino's son, trying to spoil his image business. They would buy no images because they worshiped a terrible god of their own. And these were Christians, and the woman was leading them nearer and nearer to the crowd.

In the midst of the green was a small house which seemed the center of everything. The little bell rang from within it. It was a flimsy house built of wattles, or willow wands, and roofed with thatch. Morning-glory vines twined up the sides and flowered on sides and thatch. It was noon now, time for the flowers to close, but they were still open in the coolness.

Lavinia looked about for the altar of sacrifice but saw none. Perhaps the foul thing was hidden in the house of wattles and already reeking with blood. The Christian worship was always hidden. In Rome it was in caves and cellars. By this time Lavinia was so frightened that her tongue was dry and fear was like anger in her breast. For fear and anger are one.

Now a company of boys came forth from a house on the edge of the green. They formed themselves into a procession and began to sing in the clear white tone of boyish voices. But fear was like a curtain between Lavinia's mind and all beauty. She scarcely heard them. They were marching toward the house of wattles. Ah, Govan was at their head. As she saw

Govan her fear abated. How could anyone so kind do harm to her or to Mother. His eyes looked hither and yon until he found her. Then he smiled. Now Govan's mother, whom the people called Camilla, took her hand and Aurelia's and led them with the crowd into the little house. Soon the room was choked with people, but there were more people outside standing with faces toward the house. The door was wide open. That was the only light. The boys had ceased singing.

Fearfully Lavinia looked again for the altar of sacrifice but again there was none—no, not anywhere. Only a small table covered with a pure white cloth, and on it a plain silver cup and loaves of bread piled up. The smell of the fresh bread filled the room. Relief surged through her. If there was no altar this could not be religious worship, for no one came to a god without a gift—even if it were only a small cake. How could they burn the bread on that pure white cloth? How could they kill anyone on top of that little table? And the priest had no knife.

"Mother," she whispered, "there is no altar."

"No," said Aurelia, "I think it is a feast. Perhaps a springtime festival."

Now to their surprise Camilla stepped forward—as much as she could for the crowd. She lifted her hands in the old attitude of prayer.

"Oh, God," she began, "teach us to love Thee even as Thou lovest us. Teach us. Teach us. We can learn of Thee. We cannot give as Thou givest—Thy Son, Thy blessed Son. But we can receive and today we receive Thee."

She spoke passionately as if to someone in the room. Could this be a prayer? Aurelia and Lavinia looked at each other in amazement. Camilla had spoken in Latin, as if to make sure that these guests would understand.

As Camilla finished the people's voices swept in as if taking up a song and began to recite something in their native Celtic. What the people said they seemed to know by heart. One would begin at the back of the room or the old man at the table would begin and all would join. Their voices rang almost like music.

Lavinia strained not her ears but her understanding to catch the Celtic. She had perforce learned much of it in her four years in Britain. This was an unaccustomed dialect, but as it went on and on she forgot that the tongue was strange to her. Lavinia was not sensitive to sculpture but she was sensitive to poetry and to music. And she was listening now to the greatest poetry ever spoken by human lips.

"If I ascend up into heaven Thou art there; if I make my bed in Hades, behold Thou art there. If I take the wings of the morning and dwell in the uttermost parts of the sea even there shall Thy hand hold me and Thy right hand shall lead me."

"Whose hand?" thought Lavinia. "Who will lead them?"

And now the old man near the table began another:

"And now is Christ risen from the dead and become the first fruits of them that slept. If of ourselves we all die, even so in Christ shall all be made alive."

Oh, who could understand such strange wild words? Yet they were so surpassingly lovely that some harp within her quivered to their music. She looked toward her mother but Aurelia seemed wrapped in amazement. Gone far and far was fear. For fear cannot live in the presence of beauty.

And now Govan's voice lifted in song, and the boys immediately joined him, high and clear. It was not like a religious song. Indeed, it was a Celtic folk song imbued, as folk song is, with the soul of a whole people. It seemed a greeting to someone called Jesus. The tune was rhythmic and vigorous. It kept to no humdrum tonality but stepped from grave to gay, rested where no rest was, and began again. What a tune! And how masterly was Govan's voice in the lead—a voice effortless in power and full of a sort of rightness that Lavinia had never heard before. Sometimes he sang with the boys; sometimes his voice winged forth in a melody of its own—yes, like a bird. It was plain he was singing this melody of himself and for the first time. Yet winging in and out of the chorus, it was always in harmony.

Lavinia looked toward Govan. Ah, he was gazing straight at her. She was so startled that the harp that was her spirit twanged again. Oh, surely it was as if she, too, were singing with him. How blue his eyes were. And how beautiful he was, to be sure, tall and arrow straight. He had saved her and saved Mother and now he was saving her again from her fear. Oh, what was this? No one had ever bent that look upon her. It searched her soul. Yet kindness was in it, kindness and nearness and truth. He must not look at her in this way. He must look elsewhere. Yet if he did . . .

The song ceased and Lavinia came to herself. But she felt as if she had been snatched bodily into the air. Nor did she fully come down again.

Then after a long quietness the old priest began to pray. Then others prayed aloud, even quite young persons as the hearts overflowed in prayer. There was one prayer addressed to the Lord of the heavens as if they were addressing Jupiter. But the rest of the prayer could not possibly be to Jupiter, and in all the prayers was a confidence, yea, and a sort of intimacy with their god which to the pagan Lavinia was almost fearful to hear.

And now the old man at the table began to tell a story.

He spoke in Latin and Lavinia realized that it was because he wanted her and Aurelia to understand. This story, too, was strange though simple enough. It was about twelve friends and One other who were taking supper together. The enemies of that One were all near about and were going to kill him. And at the supper this One gave bread and wine to his friends. And He told them he was dying for their sakes and that they must always drink the wine and eat the bread in remembrance of Him. "My body is broken for you," He said. "My blood is shed for you."

"And now we," the old man finished, "we are His friends, nay, as branches of the vine that is Himself—we also come to our Savior's feast and we know that He is with us."

After this there was no speaking, only silence and action. Govan filled the silver cup with wine and the old man came, giving it to everyone in turn. Govan followed with a basket of bread, giving a small loaf to each person. Not only did they give to those in church but went out the door to those who were outside. The people did not sip but drank. Govan had to fill the cup again and again. Little children were lifted that they might drink. The people sitting on the ground rose in a sort of joyous reverence as the cup came toward them. It almost seemed to Lavinia that they were worshiping the cup. But surely they would not do that. How happy they were in their feast. Never had Lavinia seen such shining faces— never at any feast or household rejoicing. What was this joy as of hearts set free? As if they lived somewhere beyond all harm or fear of it? After the cup and basket were brought back to the table, these people did the strangest thing of all. Each person kissed the one next him—be it man, woman, or child—reverently, respectfully.

"It is the kiss of Peace," whispered Camilla.

Suddenly, quite suddenly it was all over. The people began to pour out of the church and to disperse on the green where a feast was spread. Some had brought their own food. But food seemed to be given by the people of Avalonia. And it appeared that it was to the poor and slaves that food was given. Near the house of wattles was a round hut of stone domed with a hole atop. Smoke poured from it and a smell of cooking like heavy incense.

Lavinia now stood in the open sunshine. The happy people were all about her, laughing, greeting each other, inviting each other to the feast. Lavinia realized that she was very hungry. Oh, more than that, she was very lonely. As high as her spirit had soared now was it low. She had never been lonely like this. It made no difference that Mother was near her—no difference at all. For of course *he* would never come—Govan would not. Why would he care to see her again? She who was so homely that Decimus had given up all he possessed rather than bear the sight of her. Minutes passed, long, long minutes, and more than minutes. No, of course he would not come. He would never come.

Then suddenly at a run there he was coming, coming. Yes—and to her. He was here! And yes, he was just as beautiful as he had been in the house there. He was flushed and out of breath.

"Did you like it?" he was demanding. "Did you understand? Part of it was in Latin. Surely you understood. Tell me. Why don't you speak?"

He seized both her hands, shaking her as if to waken her—but she could not answer him. She could only watch his eyes and the deep beauty in them and his quick, quick ways.

"Oh, you funny child. I believe you understood everything." He laughed.

CHAPTER TWENTY-FOUR

She found voice at last:

"What was it? It was strange and beautiful. Why do they say those things?"

"I will tell you," he said excitedly, "for you do want to know. Do you not?"

She wanted to know anything that Govan could tell her. Any words that he might speak; if only she could be near him and hear him speaking it was enough.

"But first we will have our feast—all of us together," he went on. He turned to Aurelia. "It is the feast of our Risen Lord. I made them wait until you and your daughter could come to it."

"I thank you," Aurelia answered. "Indeed, we have so much to thank you for. Both you and your mother, Camilla."

He still held Lavinia's hand, leading her and the others to where his feast was spread.

"Tell me your name," he said so low that only she could hear. "It is dreadful not to know your name."

CHAPTER TWENTY-FIVE

HERE ARE some hours so golden and alight that they do not slip back into the abyss of time, but stay always clear and living in the mind. Perhaps such hours follow us even into heaven and there our souls can relive them, not as memory but as actual rooms into which we can enter. For in heaven imagination becomes reality.

Such an hour was this which Lavinia now approached, oh, a number of hours, like precious pearls on a string.

First was the Resurrection Feast of which she and Govan with Aurelia and Camilla partook, sitting on the ground with the wholesome food set in dishes on the grass. Govan kept springing up from the repast—most impolite since he was their host. But once it was to serve a poor ragged man who stood looking lost; again the boys one after another came to him. The boys seemed to depend upon him for everything and the rest of the village was not much better.

"We feed the poor folk round about whether they be Christians or not," Camilla explained.

"But why?" Aurelia inquired. "Are you really so afraid of

them? Must you keep them contented?"

"Oh no—no." Camilla laughed. "It is the wish of our Savior and all our church helps the poor."

Charity was not unknown in Rome but it was exceedingly rare. Both Aurelia and Lavinia were puzzled. Now Govan returned, throwing himself breathlessly upon the grass.

"Isn't our Avalonia beautiful today?" he exclaimed.

Lavinia smiled. How could anyone think that of a place with no marble temples, no triumphal arches or straight streets? Govan had spoken to Aurelia but he was always aware of Lavinia.

"But you must see it is beautiful," he urged. "The little houses underneath the trees, the laburnum flowering and the eglantine blooming on the thatched roofs, and the air about us so clear and quiet."

Her smile trilled into laughter, but it was because somehow she caught the beauty he had meant, and it was lovely and contenting to her mind.

They finished the meal slowly and it was late afternoon when Aurelia rose to go back to the hut.

"Let your daughter stay," pleaded Govan. "The sunshine is so golden now."

Aurelia glanced back at the hut and like a prudent Roman mother realized that she could watch her daughter from the doorway. She consented. Immediately when she and Camilla were gone a silence fell. Lavinia could not break it, and it seemed Govan did not want to break it. He sat, looking her up and down, that clear, appraising look that was half inquiry, as if he were going deeper, deeper into knowledge of her. For a moment Lavinia thought of her rough dress, of her face so despised by Decimus, but this self-consciousness faded before the intimacy of his gaze. He was speaking now:

"I can hardly believe you are the same person I found in the wood yesterday. So bedraggled, so soaking wet. It must have rained torrents where you had been."

"It wasn't just the rain," she said.

"What else then?"

"Mother and I jumped into a stream. We—well, we tried to kill ourselves to get away from the Durotrigs."

He cried out as if she had struck him. He seized her hand.

"Oh, I was not brave to die," confessed Lavinia. "I wanted to live, to live."

"Then," said Govan quietly, "it was that I heard. I understand now."

"But we did not cry out—not either of us. We—we just jumped in." Lavinia shuddered. "You could not have heard."

He spoke again in a low voice.

"It wasn't outward hearing. But it was a cry that reached me."

It was Lavinia's turn to gaze. Was the young man crazy?

"Many of us are able to hear that way, not all. But I am one who hears. Our Lord opens the door of the spirit and I see through."

"But I thought you said you *heard*," she queried desperately.

"It is all the same," he answered, smiling at her as if she were the smallest child. He held her hand closer in his warm clasp.

"We had been to Moridunum to the ship and had fetched the bags of grain. We were walking our horses up a hill on the Fosse Way—when my horse stopped and there in that quiet my whole heart was flooded with a sense of need, of pain like pain in my own breast. It was you, but I thought only of Avalonia. I told Lucius and he, too, said I was crazy." (He smiled at her a teasing smile.) "He said, 'Avalonia is far away,' and that I was possessed. But I made them all hurry. Hours passed and how they laughed at me. Then we came to the overturned *raeda,* all sorts of things scattered on the road. My men stopped laughing. And not long after we came to the little path which the Durotrigs always use, and by the goodness of God we took it. Then at last we came upon you."

"Oh, Govan, Govan, I will never think you were crazy," cried Lavinia. Suddenly it was terrible to her that she had so misunderstood him, that something in him and about him was completely beyond her ken.

"What does it mean, all the impossible things that people do here, and the strange, strange things they say and you say? You are not like us—not like anyone I ever knew."

He edged nearer to her, still holding her hand, his face eager as if she had just given him a gift.

"Do you want to know? Will you let me tell you?" he demanded.

"Yes," she whispered, awed and a little afraid.

"It is because we are living a new life. It is a life that was brought down from high heaven by one in whom was the fullness of God. He died about ninety years ago. He was a Jew named Jesus. He is more beautiful to me than moonlight or sunrise, more precious than sight itself. If He came to us now (and He does that sometimes), if He came walking toward us over the green grass, I would run toward Him and kiss the hem of His garment."

Her amazed face brought him to himself.

"I must tell you carefully—forgive me—carefully so you will understand."

Then Govan began to tell the Christ story which went deeper and deeper in unbelievableness until it was over her head entirely. When Govan said, "Crucified," she cried out:

"But that is a shameful death. Only for common criminals. I can't imagine loving anyone who had been crucified!"

"I can," he said. "I imagine Him and love Him every day. But I do not imagine His death but His living again. It was only three days till He came alive."

"Came alive!" she repeated.

"Yes. He makes our life to be full of joy and even in death we are not afraid."

"Do you mean to say that if I had drowned myself I would still be alive?" she demanded.

"Yes, dear child, I mean to say that."

Abruptly he stopped. The wild story had affrighted the heathen mind. He sprang up from the ground, pulling her up with him.

"There! I've done it again! I always tell too much. Forget it, dear child, because," he added inconsequently, "you will not forget it. He will come to you at need. Now I will show you our beautiful town that is not beautiful."

"I will always love it," she said passionately. "Wherever I am, however far away, I will always remember it."

They were walking across the green, still hand in hand. The people were dispersing now, some into the houses, some going down the steep hill toward the marsh and mere. Govan showed her the thorn tree that bloomed on the birthday of their Lord. He showed her the cup in the little house of wattles and told her that a man named Joseph of Arimathaea had brought it and that Jesus had drunk of it at the Last Supper. He told her how this Joseph had come with twelve followers to tell the people of Britain about Jesus. He showed her the house where the followers of this first twelve lived.

"They are always twelve," he told her, "because our Lord had twelve men whom he taught. But if they marry, they live in one of the other houses." He showed her the house of the boys where he taught them and cared for them.

"Sometimes the boys are poor and clothed in rags when they first come. I was when I came."

"But, Govan, I thought you were born here."

"No, I was born in Isca Salures," he answered.

"Oh," she said, "that's where my father is. He is *legatus legiones.*"

"Is he? Is he?" Govan questioned, delighted. "My father was *tribunus militum* in the Second. Oh, that will make it easier for us."

She blushed crimson, knowing well what he meant. But would anything make it easier for them? Was she not as good as promised to Carminius? Did Father ever break a promise? A dark shadow of despair crossed her. She had not realized till this moment that she was thinking of Govan as her lover. But—of course she was, and if lover, why not more than that? She had never expected marriage as coming by this road. Marriage was a duty to Father. She had known that always. Oh, what was she thinking about? Govan was talking and she did not even hear what he said.

"I love you when you are rosy like that and all confused." He laughed. "But I loved you when you were all drowned and bedraggled and sitting on the donkey."

"How could you?" was her wondering answer. And how could Govan be so light-hearted, expecting no difficulty anywhere. But somehow he made her hopeful too.

"This is Weary All Hill," he was telling her. "Ah, I was weary all when I first climbed up it."

"Come back to where we were sitting while I tell you about myself and how I came to Avalon." So he said and led her back to the grass on the edge of the hill.

She was aware of a charming vanity in him—a vanity that came somehow from his appreciation of life. The world about him was so bright to Govan that he himself was bright in the midst of it.

"My father was a Roman officer from Pisae," he began. "My mother is a Silurian from the mountains. But very early my father was killed in a skirmish and then gradually we became very poor. I was a thoroughly naughty boy." (Govan seemed greatly to relish this.) "I was the head of a gang of small boys. Well, somehow I got into a fight with the leader of the other gang. I beat him" (this also Govan relished), "but not before he had rolled me in the dirt and scratched my face and eyes and gotten my eyes filled with the dirt. Then my eyes did not get better. Oh, how I suffered and how my dear mother suffered with me! Gradually, gradually—shall I ever forget that darkening?—the light left me and I saw no more."

"Oh," she cried out. "You were not blind! Not your eyes so bright as they are!"

"Blind as a bat that flies in the night, and blinder yet in my heart. I was furious and beat with my fists. I was melancholy and sat for hours in a stupor. My poor mother was beside herself for I was as I am now, the idol of her heart. Then she heard of a man at a far-away place called Avalonia who could cure people of blindness. And leading me, she started out to find him. Oh, so long, so long was the way! And sometimes she had to carry me on her back, big boy that I was. She never lost courage but I had had none to begin with. When we reached the bottom of this hill we were two beggars with the rags scarce clinging to us. How we climbed up I will never know. Then we stood before the old man. He was the son of Joseph of Arimathaea and was also named Joseph. His voice soothed me at once. His voice was a light even before he brought the light to my eyes. It was from his lips that I first heard the name of my Lord.

"The kind women of Avalon cared for my mother, and Joseph led me to his own house and laid me on his bed. He sat beside me and rebuked my blindness. He told me that Jesus would come to my help. Then he sat silent and I went to sleep. I was awakened by his hands on my face and hearing his fervent voice. Then suddenly I seemed to see stars pouring down the close curtains of my darkness, tongues of flame that did not burn. He took his hands away. 'Open your eyes,' he said.

"I opened them and saw. I saw the old man, the little room with the flickering candle in it. Will I ever forget that candle? I leaped from the bed, fell on my knees before him, and clasped his feet and thanked and thanked him. I don't suppose he understood, for I spoke my rude mountain dialect. Then I ran out the door into the night. 'Where is the east?' I cried to everyone I met. 'Where is the east?'

"And when they told me, I ran to the edge of the hill and sat down and looked at the sky. And behold, the stars rose one after the other, red stars, blue stars, and at last the morning star, heralding the sun. It was then I began to sing. I did not think of it as singing but as greeting that star. No Magus following to Bethlehem ever loved his star as I did that star of the morning. The people in the town heard my singing and came and stood about me, but I did not know they were there. They say my chant was beautiful but I do not remember it, for the Lord sang through me at that time. I sang and sang until the sun rose in wide and golden glory. Then I was silent and presently I slept, and they carried me to my mother."

When Govan had finished his tale the sun had set and the

miracle of silver light possessed the sky and earth. The moon rose like a disk of pure glass, only half lighted because of the pervasive twilight.

Perhaps it was the quiet light that freed Lavinia from her shyness, for she found herself telling Govan about Marcus, about her own journeys through many lands, of her arrival in Britain.

"And in all those journeys you were coming to me—to me," he rejoiced.

Talking or in silence, they sat together until Aurelia came to tell them that the evening was far spent and that Lavinia must come at once.

They rose in silence from the dewy grass. Govan put both arms about Lavinia and kissed her twice, nay three times. And Aurelia thought it was high time she had summoned her daughter.

Chapter Twenty-Six

THEY STARTED next morning in the first gold of dawn. Marcia had left for her home on the afternoon before.

Down the steep hill of Avalonia they went to the marsh country. Lavinia felt that she could not have borne to leave the place where she had been so happy had not Govan been going with them, to take them home and stay a while under their roof. She looked back to where the uplifted hill caught the first golden light of dawn. But she could not see that more mysterious dawn which was caught by the Glistening Island. A dawn which was to spread all over Britain, filling it with new light, giving it spires of cathedral beauty and in the hearts of men purpose, strength, and hope.

Sometimes Govan rode next to Aurelia but oftener near to Lavinia. In the slow walk of the horses on the lonely road there was no end of what these two wanted to say to each other. By nightfall they came to Aqua Sulis, stayed the night at an inn at the edge of town, and started next morning for Corinium.

It was still early when Lavinia observed a party far up the road hurrying toward them at a gallop.

"Mother," she called, "that white horse looks like the one Duris rides, and, oh, that big horse gallops like Father's."

Before she could finish the horsemen were among them. Favonius indeed it was. His face was wild, his hair matted on his forehead. He peered at the strangers, recognized his wife among them, gasped, and his face changed to joy, or was it wrath?

"Favonius," cried out Aurelia. But he had already driven his horse flank to flank by hers. He seized her by both shoulders, gazing at her.

"Aurelia! Are you safe? Are you unharmed? How did you get away from the robbers? Lavinia. Where is my daughter?"

"She is here. See, right here. I am all well. We are both unharmed."

He seemed to believe her yet not believe her. He shook her roughly.

"How dared you go off without asking me? How dared you run away from me?"

"Favonius! Oh, I didn't run away. Oh, oh, I am so sorry!"

It seemed impossible that even her husband dared shake a dignified lady as Favonius was shaking his wife.

"I have been crazy, I tell you—I have been like a maniac. I came down to get the remainder of my legion. The whole north is in rebellion."

"Listen, only listen to me," pleaded Aurelia as well as she could between chattering teeth.

"I stopped at Aqua Sulis for a glimpse of you. I had no time even for that. There I heard. *Taken by robbers!* I have been home. I have dispatched men down the Fosse Way after you. I have lost precious time with my legion. I can't stop with you now."

He let fall his hands. The relief had gradually seeped into

his soul. He tightened the reins of his horse.

"I must go," he said. "Come back to Aqua Sulis with me."

Aurelia was white with humiliation, yes, and repentance.

"Oh, I wouldn't have done this to you for the whole world," she began.

"How did you get safe?" he demanded. "Was it true about the robbers?"

"Yes—we were taken. And this young man here saved us. He fought the whole troop of them. Govan," she called.

Govan drove forward. He could but think this father of Lavinia's was a wild man. What a way to treat a wife! He was a brute.

Then Favonius did the worst thing of all. He was in no clear mood to estimate Govan. Govan seemed to him a poor native young man, rough clad.

"Young man," said Favonius, "I am eternally in your debt. I shall reward you. My wife shall have to see to it. A generous amount. It can't be too generous."

Now Govan, for all the humble teachings of his faith, had pride. It was the overweening pride of the Celt, inherited from his Celtish mother. Through all his life Govan was hardly to overcome it. Reward him with money for an act of valor, for saving two people who had become intensely dear to him! Govan's face went crimson.

"I wish no money, sir, for doing what was my common duty," he said, and he wheeled his horse about.

"What's this? What's this?" exclaimed Favonius. Was it possible that the *legatus* of a legion was being addressed in this fashion? Favonius could hardly believe what he heard.

"Oh, Govan, don't be angry," put in Aurelia. "My husband does not understand."

"But I understand only too well," was Govan's answer.

There was no time for explanation. Favonius was mad with haste. Aurelia beside herself with desire to quiet him. Govan was, after all, right in his instinct that this was no time to burden himself upon the disturbed family. He moved his horse to Lavinia's, and there to Favonius' aghast amazement put his arm about the girl, drew her toward him, and kissed her three times with fervor, calling her by some endearing Celtish word as if Latin endearments were all too faint for his love.

Then he and his men galloped away toward the west.

The time at Aqua Sulis was short. Within an hour Favonius was hurrying toward Glevum whither the cohorts of his Legion Augusta were supposed to be marching to meet him. Aurelia, Lavinia, and their maids went at once to Corinium where Aurelia had to search the city for the fastest horsemen to go down the Fosse Way and fetch back the rescuers whom Favonius had sent forth. The fighting in the north stirred all Corinium with anxiety, for many had sons, brothers, and husbands at the front.

Poor Lavinia, caught between the bad tempers of two men, knew not what to do. She moved about her home duties as if in a dream. If only Father had not been so furious; if only Govan had not flared up so quick and fiery.

At first she expected Govan to come riding back to her. But he did not come. A week passed and he did not come. Two weeks, and still she kept watching the front gate, fluttered at every footstep there. Could he have kissed her as he had done right before Father and yet forget her? She had heard that men did so. And yet Govan? Surely she could trust Govan. But he should not have kissed her before Father the way he did. Father would be angry forever and ever. No chance now for forgiveness. But, oh, suppose he had not kissed her then, and she would not have that to remember and remember. Oh, Govan had done right.

Meanwhile she was in mortal fear of Carminius. He would come to see her, taking the marriage for granted. They were as good as promised. It had been bad enough to think of this when she had not known Govan. But now to marry Carminius was a desecration. All night she would weep with only snatches of slumber. By day go stealing about the house like a ghost of Lavinia.

"Daughter, don't take it so hard," pleaded Aurelia. "We all have trials; we all must face them."

"But, Mother, don't you love Govan too? Say that you love him."

Aurelia smiled.

"He is an incorrigible young man but it would be impossible not to love him."

"Would you—" began Lavinia, then began again.

"Yes, dear child, strange as it may seem, I would let you marry him. But Father, I don't know about your father. And we must not forget Carminius."

So the trouble settled down again as black as ever.

Then like the stroke of a sword came something that made all other troubles as vain shadows.

She heard first Buvinda keening and wailing in the garden, running, running with the news as if glad to kill all gladness.

"Young Master is dead. Young Master is dead." Aurelia came running from the house, seized Buvinda, and shook her.

"Hush, where did you hear it?"

"Oh, it's true, it's true. The messenger!"

And there was the messenger, standing as if guilty, weeping as if he himself were dealing the blow. He was from Favonius himself. He had no letter, only the dreadful tidings. Marcus Claudius—yes, Marcus was dead. The whole Ninth Legion had been cut to pieces. It no more existed.

Lavinia had hurried to her mother. She was so stunned that nothing was real to her. She was afraid to touch her mother. Then she threw both arms about her.

"Come into the house," said Aurelia to the messenger. "Tell us all you know."

She put her arm about Lavinia and together they walked into the tablinium. As Lavinia caught sight of the altar and the images which she and Marcus had set up together, a broken-hearted cry passed her lips, but she choked it back. Lavinia had the instinct of all who live closely in families. The sorrow was not first her own. It was Mother's. Her's came afterward. Yes, afterward. Aurelia questioned and requestioned the man but he could tell her little more. Just that Favonius had summoned him to his tent and sent him with the news. Just that Favonius himself and all men at the front were in danger. The man was exhausted with his long ride, half asleep on his feet. Aurelia called a slave to serve him, herself led him to a room and bade him rest. She lingered over each task, but at last she had to come back to the tablinium, at last had to sit there in silence, pressing her daughter's hand until Lavinia's hand ached with the grasp.

"I wish I were with your father," she kept saying, and Lavinia knew it was because she was wanting to help him.

CHAPTER TWENTY-SEVEN

HOW did those days ever pass! Lavinia did not know. She only knew that with every hour the hurt grew deeper, took on new aspects of loss. Now it was Marcus coming to her room, summoning her on that winter morning. Such a rosy face. Now it was Marcus in full armor as she last saw him. Marcus! Marcus! All the way back to his little boyhood in Rome when she helped him with his lessons. Then she would forget he was dead. Only to remember it again.

People came flocking to the house, neighbors and people they scarcely knew. All wailing or beating their breasts. There could be no burial! How they harped upon that. Marcus' ghost would wander forever. Marcus' ghost! How could Marcus, so swift, so full of life, be a ghost? Carminius came. He clasped her hand and kissed her forehead but she did not care whether he touched her or not. She hardly knew he was there.

Then one morning she began to long for Govan. For Mother's sake she wanted him at first. Somehow she knew that Govan would be steady and strong. He would not wail and make things worse. What was that curious thing he had said to her, that if she had been drowned in the stream she would still be alive? Maybe he would say that to Mother about Marcus. Maybe that would somehow be a comfort to Mother.

Then her thought veered like a gale to herself. For herself she wanted Govan, for herself to hear him say that strange thing again. What if it could not be true? She wanted to hear him say it. Govan must come. All fear that he was unfaithful or had forgotten left her. She could feel his warm hand as it upheld her on the donkey. She could feel his arm about her, holding the cloak so close, keeping her from falling when she could no longer sit up.

"Come," she said aloud. Sitting stiff like a hieratic statue on the edge of the bed—her hands clenched at her side.

She must make him come, but how? How reach out to him when he was so far away? What could she do? Lavinia knew when people wanted a boon and had no other way to get it they offered things to the gods. The gods then might pay back. What a relief—to have something to do.

She hurried to the storehouse, got the best honey, the freshest cakes, her father's choicest wine. She stole into the tablinium like a thief. Nobody must see her. This was her sacrifice to bring Govan—hers only—to fetch him quickly. Should it be to Vesta? Yes, for Vesta cared for the home, and if Govan came he could comfort the home that had been so cruelly wounded. She heaped up the gifts in front of Vesta. Oh, Vesta, behold, behold. She poured out the wine on the floor. She stood with hands uplifted.

"Aunt Aurelia in Rome is your own Vestal Virgin," she told the goddess. "She is my aunt and has served you all her life. If you won't do it for me do it for her."

She stood long and long in silence. Then went to her room and lay down. The golden chain that dear Marcus had given her was about her neck. She fingered the moon on it; she fingered the tiny gold sun. It was a charm. It must work. So she lay until nightfall when she went to sleep.

She awoke next morning more in fear than hope. No, Govan had not come. All day she waited; she put more gifts at Vesta's feet. One could hardly see the little image on the altar for the gifts piled about it. But that day passed and the next and somehow the dull silence at the gate made her know that her prayer was not answered. Vesta did not care. Well she must try another god—a bigger gift. Something more difficult.

There was the temple to Jupiter Optimus Maximus in the Forum. Lavinia had never gone there by herself. Such sacrifices were family doings—everyone together. And Father bought the ram. Lavinia had no money. It had never seemed necessary that she should. But now she went to her mother and asked for money. Aurelia, thinking it was for some household necessity, gave it to her. She was too sorrowful to be curious about anything.

Lavinia was very timid about this errand. But very secret too. She brought Stephana, her maid. Together they went to the sheep market which, of course, was next to the temple. Together they found their way to the priest and paid him for the sacrifice, together they followed him to the great altar which was in front of the temple. Lavinia did not think about Stephana being with her. Stephana was only a slave. Lavinia was alone—alone with her insistent prayer that Govan must come.

The old priest went through all the forms. He mumbled and mumbled. It was not necessary that Lavinia should hear. She covered her head as was required. She looked nowhere for fear of seeing some bad luck. But just as the priest laid the sheep on the altar, pushed back its head and severed its neck, Lavinia, by some horrible revulsion, she knew not what, lifted her veil and looked.

She screamed at the sight as if she herself were the sheep.

"Silence," thundered the priest. "What evil are you doing! Leave the altar. Go."

But he had no need to command her. Lavinia seized Stephana's hand and fled as from evil itself, sobbing now uncontrollably in the street, running for home, to hide herself. To hide herself.

Fortunately Mother was in the farthest part of the house and did not hear her. For Lavinia kept on sobbing with a wildness she could not stop. She hid herself in her room. All her life she had attended such sacrifice but she had never looked. She had never cared about the sheep. Anyway, why should Jupiter want a sheep? Could a god smell the mutton when it was burned? What cruel things Jupiter did! She hated Jupiter. What was the matter with her? Was she going stark mad?

A thought kept teasing at her mind, unable to get in for her wildness and confusion. What was it? As she quieted down, it came clear. It was something Govan had said:

"Our Lord has cleansed the altars of the world. There shall be no more blood spilt upon them."

Well, she would never again go to an altar of blood. Never.

But Govan had told her why. She wished she had listened more carefully. She had been always looking at Govan's face and thinking how beautiful he was. What had he said?

"Our God needs no gifts and no urging. Our God comes on running feet. He makes our life to be full of joy and even in death we are not afraid."

Could that be? Could anybody not be afraid of death?

She rose hastily as if seeking something she could grasp with her hands. She went out of the room, out through the garden gate and into the wood where she and Marcus had been so happy on that winter morning of snow. Now the wood was freshly green and very quiet. She walked far into the shadowy aisles, then turned and came again toward home. Lavinia had never made decisions. Those had always been made for her. It did not occur to her that she could turn her back upon the gods of her race, turn her back upon her family and all its proud traditions. Ay, turn her back upon Rome itself.

She did not decide now. But just at the edge of the wood she stopped, faced the woodland quiet, lifted her hands high as Romans did, and began to pray to the god who comes on running feet. She prayed only for Govan to come. But she did not snatch and insist. Her whole soul waited because this god had running feet and must come of Himself. She did not know how long she stood there. Perhaps a moment, perhaps an hour.

She heard no footsteps behind her, but immediately warm arms were about her, a cheek pressed against her own. And now Govan turned her about and she saw his face. He did not wait for her question but began to speak in a low, quiet voice.

"Marcus is not in the dark. If you could see his morning and his sunlight you would sing for joy."

"Yes, yes," she whispered, but it was not an assent but an insistance that he say more.

"Our Lord conquered death. It was with love that He conquered it. Only love could have such power. Don't imagine you can love Marcus as our Lord does. Don't imagine that."

So he went on and on. Sometimes keeping silence, sometimes speaking, while upon her mind, parched with grief, came a freshness and a fragrance as of rain. And at last came—trust. Slowly, slowly her faith flowered into ecstasy, and he watched it as it flowered and bloomed.

CHAPTER TWENTY-EIGHT

S THEY were walking back to the house, Lavinia said to Govan: "Don't tell Mother. Don't tell her what I believe."

"No," he answered. "I shall do nothing to grieve her or startle her."

But after all it was Aurelia who startled them. They had finished the evening meal. Lavinia rose from her place, came and sat on her mother's footstool, leaning against her knee and looking up wistfully as if she were asking some forgiveness. A whimsical smile changed for a moment the settled sadness of Aurelia's face.

"Well, daughter," she said. "Tell me. I think I know well what you want to say."

"Oh, Mother, Mother," wept Lavinia, clasping her mother's arm. "I am not going to desert you. I will never do that."

"But you have embraced the new faith. I knew it the instant you entered the room."

Lavinia hid her face, quivering. This was a momentous change to step from the old to the new. Pain was sure to follow. Then Aurelia said:

"You cannot desert me, dear child. I have been a Christian ever since our day in Avalonia."

Lavinia cried out with joy:

"Why didn't you tell me? Why didn't you tell me?"

"I would not persuade my husband's daughter away from him. Sorrow enough is his."

Govan came to them, throwing his arms about them both together.

"Aurelia," he said, "I believe you are a natural Christian. The door was always half open to you."

His was partly the saintly joy of knowing a new convert to the faith, but it was also the worldly joy that now he could almost surely have Lavinia for his own.

It was a well-nigh happy evening, an hour snatched from grief into comforting and contentment.

Govan told them why he had not come long ago. On his return to Avalonia, he found awaiting him an urgent mission to go to the end of the western peninsula to help some new converts there.

"A just punishment for me," said he. "For I was hardly started on the journey when I repented me of my anger against Favonius. I longed to hasten here and it was torture to be going in the other direction."

He had returned at last to his home, there to hear that the Ninth Legion had been cut to pieces. Lavinia's brother was in the Ninth Legion. So she had told him. And now his horse could not gallop fast enough to Corinium. At the outer gate of the city his worst fear was confirmed. And as he neared Lavinia's home, he saw her standing alone by the wood.

Then after he had told of his joy in that meeting Govan began to tell them stories. They were stories he had learned from travelers who came from the land where the Lord had lived. There was a story of a woman who went early in the morning to the Lord's tomb and found it empty. There was the story of the two men walking to Emmaus whom the Lord met but they did not know Him. Only when He sat at table with them and broke bread so familiarly did they recognise Him who had died three days before.

There was the story of the young man cured of his blindness, whose parents turned against him and whose people cast him out because he kept asserting that the Lord had done it.

There was the story of Jesus the night before His death who, though He knew His enemies were coming with swords and staves for to kill Him, yet said to His friends:

"Fear not, I have overcome the world."

Aurelia and Lavinia had never heard these stories. They did not know either their beginning nor their end. Even the slaves who passed through the room on errands stopped to hear how the stories turned out. Aurelia did not send them away.

It was late when the three parted for the night. And it seemed as if they had been in another country.

There in the house of grief Govan indeed came like a lighted candle. For of course he stayed, lifting burdens from Aurelia, managing the household, meeting friends so Aurelia, in the exhaustion that follows grief, might be quiet and have rest. Lavinia dreaded her father's coming, but even when he came there was no disturbance. He was too grief-stricken, too worn out with the long fighting in the north to criticize anything or even to wonder at Govan's presence. The tribes of the north were at last subdued. But at a fearful price. The Ninth Legion was annihilated. There was no such legion any more.

He marveled at Aurelia's strength and himself took

strength from hers, little knowing the source whence it came.

Even Lavinia's marriage did not concern him now, nor did it occur to him to associate Govan with such an event.

Slowly the weeks passed in the shadow of the new grief. Again and again the new faith fought with that sorrow, now winning, now taking defeat. But for Lavinia each defeat seemed to give the faith fresh power. Out of the deep valley she would suddenly mount to a height of exaltation—a sense of relationship with Marcus which she had never had before.

"He is my brother," she would say; "he understands me now."

Of all the household only Govan was really busy. He seemed to have some growing occupation in the town. People were constantly coming to see him, poor slaves or young men of standing, mothers with their children, often sick children, in their arms. These he would meet in the wood near the house, stay with them for hours or even return with them to their homes. But Lavinia knew why he lingered in Corinium.

"I will never leave without you," he told her.

"But Father has not consented," she answered desperately. "He has not even thought it possible that—"

"That you should belong to me." He finished her sentence. "Darling Lavinia, that is only his blindness. For you do belong to me. Always—ever since you were a little girl in Rome you have been mine. Don't you understand? God would not have given me knowledge of you there on the highroad while you were yet unseen—no, He would not if He had not intended you for me. Don't be afraid."

And with his arm close about her and his bright face gazing into hers she could not be afraid. But the marvel still possessed her.

"Why do you love me?" she faltered. "Why?"

"Why does the sun rise?" he demanded. "Oh, Lavinia, all things are a mystery, and only the mystery of our love explains all the rest."

No wonder Lavinia went about her tasks healed of her grief, at times searching her heart for the pain that was not there.

Then late one afternoon came Buvinda to Lavinia's bedroom. Her eyes were bright with terror. Buvinda was always first to know events, be they good or bad.

"Young mistress, oh, come quick," she pleaded. "There are travelers at the gate. They are asking for Master Marcus. Oh, I don't dare go to Master Favonius. Perhaps they are from the dead."

The terror possessed Lavinia also. What could people be doing asking for Marcus? She ran quickly out into the garden and to the gate. There was a small party waiting, slaves dusty from long travel, two *raedas* with curtains drawn back and a man and a girl standing beside them. Lavinia first recognized Agathocles, their kind host at Arlate. Then she saw Neraea. She ran to her in a very excess of love.

"Oh, Neraea, Neraea!" she cried.

But the moment Neraea saw Lavinia's face she knew the truth. She began to tremble so that she could hardly stand. Lavinia, with arm close about her, led her across the garden to her own room and laid her upon the bed. Hither came Aurelia running, knelt by the bed and held Neraea in her arms.

"Oh, my child, my child," she called her, and Neraea knew that Aurelia was saying "my daughter."

"I have thought of you, yes, every day, and I wrote you a long letter. It must have passed you on the way. How good of you to come to us! But how did you know—dear heart—how did you know?"

"It was the Emperor's messenger," Neraea's trembling voice answered. "He came galloping through Arlate crying the news about the Ninth Legion. I knew Marcus belonged to it. He wrote me often—so faithful, so faithful. Of course, I could have sent a letter to you but, oh, I had to know quickly—and Father realized that, so he brought me; he brought me all the long way."

From now on all the household centered in Neraea. Lavinia was devoted to her. She never tired of telling Neraea of Marcus' love for her—how no other girl pleased him, how he was forever comparing and wishing. She took her to Marcus' room, showed her the lyre he had bought because it was like Neraea's, showed her the copy of the play *Ion* with certain parts cut out which he had taken with him, the pretty silver box in which he had kept her letters.

"All these are yours, Neraea," she told her. "They belong only to you."

Aurelia plainly called her "daughter." "You are one of us," she said. "You love him as we love him."

She prepared the daintiest dishes to tempt Neraea. It was as if she had no grief of her own in thinking of Neraea's sorrow. And as the days passed, Neraea had to feel the hopeful, vital quality in Aurelia's mood.

"It is as if to you Marcus were living," she said.

"He is living, dear child. Never think otherwise," Aurelia answered.

Only Favonius kept himself aloof. He was constant in attendance upon Agathocles. He left nothing undone to return the hospitality which Agathocles had given them in Arlate. In every way he did him honor. But to Neraea he would hardly speak. When he could avoid her presence he did so. Always he avoided her look. Aurelia was so shocked at this unfeeling that at last she spoke to him.

"I cannot bear the sight of her," Favonius broke out as if angry. "Is she not a constant reminder? Marcus reproves me through her."

"Favonius, how can you feel so—she means no reproof, surely, surely," urged Aurelia.

"If I had been wise—if I had consented to their marriage at Arlate—we might now have a son of Marcus to carry on our line—something, something of himself."

Aurelia saw now that tears were streaming down his face.

"I always thought I could bring him to a marriage," Favonius went on, "but he always slipped out of it. He seemed to hate marriage with anyone but this girl."

"But she is so lovely," said Aurelia. "Marcus was wise to love her. To me she seems one of our family."

"Yes, yes, I suppose so. And now"—he turned suddenly—"we must not delay Lavinia's wedding. Even though our line cannot be carried on, yet through her we shall have inheritance. No matter what our mourning she must be married. This time I am in earnest!"

"To whom?" faltered Aurelia.

"To Carminius, of course."

"Oh, Favonius, Favonius," Aurelia cried out almost with tears.

"What is the matter? Whom else?"

"Govan! Of course Govan," insisted Aurelia. "They love each other as Marcus and Neraea loved. Oh, don't make the same mistake again!"

"You like Govan?"

"Shall I not when he saved my life," she answered, "and my daughter's life as well?"

He looked into her eyes and she saw he was wavering

though not convinced.

"I am promised to Carminius' father," he said.

She bowed her head. Favonius could not but be aware that he was grieving her. But a legal promise meant too much to him.

Next day he visited Carminius' father. It appeared that the older son was not yet married. Carminius' father held back—the marriage of the younger son must still be put off, he said. Favonius suspected that a better match was somewhere in reserve. In sudden anger he broke the contract. He came home to find Aurelia anxiously awaiting him in the garden.

"The gods are with you and Govan," he said. "Carminius' father has not been honest with me. I have broken with him."

Aurelia said nothing of all this to Lavinia. She felt sure now that Favonius would pursue the matter to the end and the more ardently if he did it all himself. The required period of mourning was passed. There was nothing to delay him.

That afternoon Lavinia received a summons from her father. She went, trembling, to the tablinium to find him.

"Well, daughter," he began at once, "I hear you are all eagerness to be married."

Lavinia blushed scarlet. What a dreadful thing for Father to say! Surely he was angry.

"And so," he added, "you are to marry this young Govan. Shall we set the wedding day next week?"

Lavinia gasped. Her eyes widened; her blush became a rosiness of delight. She threw both her arms about her father's neck, clasping him close as a little child might do.

"Oh," she cried, "Govan always said you would."

"Govan is an impudent young fellow."

"Oh no, no, Govan trusted you. It was only I who was afraid."

"And you are not afraid now?"

"No, no, dear Father, how could I be?"

Favonius could not recognize his demure daughter in this glad and shining creature. That he was creating this gladness gave him a warmth and sense of purpose which had long been absent from him.

"Go find the young man," he commanded. "I wish to talk to him."

Like a startled deer she ran out of the room, through the garden, through the gate, until she found him. Then hand in hand they returned to Favonius. Favonius had never before really noticed Govan. Now as he looked at him he realized how well built, how full of health he was. A purpose and impulse in him as if he would arrive whither he set out.

"Govan," said Favonius, "you seem to have won the regard both of my wife and my daughter."

"I would like to win yours too," replied Govan, looking straight into Favonius' eyes.

Of course Govan's blue eyes were not so bright to Favonius as they were to Lavinia but they were bright enough. Besides, they were candid and honest.

"You will win it," declared Favonius. "Indeed, you have done so already or I would not be giving you my daughter."

Govan moved closer to Lavinia and his arm went about her. The gesture did not displease Favonius as it had before.

"And now, young man," he said, "we must attend to the betrothal. Where can I see your father?"

"You cannot see him, sir. He died years ago at Isca Salures."

"At Isca? But how?"

"Fighting at the head of his men. He was a *tribunus militum* of the Second Augusta."

"My legion! But that makes you like a blood kinsman to me.

Why in the name of the gods didn't you tell me this before?"

Favonius was half indignant, yet wholly delighted.

After this momentous decision Favonius became utterly changed toward Neraea. Aurelia could but wonder at him. Now he could not say enough in praise of Neraea. When he and Agathocles rode out Neraea had to go with them. He was delighted when he found she was a good horsewoman and gave her a pony for her own. And often he rode with her alone, talking with her freely about Marcus as he could not speak to anyone else. He told her of Marcus' easy command of men, of his fearlessness in difficult fights.

"I want her to know every phase of his character," he informed Aurelia. It seemed as if he were planning something for Neraea.

Then unexpectedly Agathocles was summoned back to Arlate. When the day came for them to go, Favonius put both hands on Neraea's shoulders, looking steadfastly into her face.

"We shall see you again," he said. "And, Neraea, if you ever marry—"

She shook her head, but Favonius went on, "I hope that you will. For I wish to adopt your first son and call him Marcus Claudius. He will belong to us, our own. Thus shall we keep our Marcus with us."

Tears filled Neraea's eyes. Adoption meant to her, as it did to all Romans, an actual entering into the adopting family, a relationship sacred, inviolable and binding as blood inheritance.

It must be noted that Neraea went back to her home bearing with her the treasure of the new faith. She had been too close to Aurelia and Lavinia not to "take knowledge of them." With her the hidden tide which had flowed up from the south into

Britain surged with renewed strength southward again.

And now all the household was changed with the preparation for Lavinia's wedding. Instead of looking backward upon death, they looked forward into life. Most of all Lavinia looked forward. Her second wedding day! But, oh, not her second but her *first,* first in joyousness, first in holiness, thrilling with light which was to shine like a lamp down all her days.

It was a Roman wedding for Favonius would have countenanced no other, and indeed, all Christians practiced the Roman ceremony. But now in all the necessary acts Govan was with her. When she went out to gather the bridal flowers Govan was beside her, watching her at the task as if she were performing some wonder. When on the eve of the bridal she put on the long *stola praetexta,* Govan must step to the doorway, gazing at her and daring not to touch. When on the wedding morning she stood at the altar in her flame-colored veil, it was Govan's strong hand that clasped hers, and when she said the ancient, fateful words: "*Quando tu Gaius, ego Gaia,*" her voice thrilled like a song.

The next day Lavinia and Govan, with full and adequate escort, journeyed the long way to Avalon. Here they received the Christian blessing of their wedding and Lavinia tasted for the first time the Christian cup. Then they returned at once to Corinium. This had been Favonius' command.

"I will buy you a villa on the White Way," he told Govan, "and there you are to live, always near us."

But to Govan the command was a miraculous fulfillment of his own wish. Was he not founding a new Christian work in Corinium? Were not many already coming through him into the presence of the Master?

* * *

Wherever you go in the south and west of England you come upon hidden saints. Sometimes there is no story, but only the name and the tiny cell or cave where the saint lived. Sometimes there is a story fragrant and unreal as a woodland flower. These are the earliest Christians of Britain, who lived long ago before the invading Saxons brought sudden night.

Govan and Lavinia of Corinium were such saints, but no tradition of them survives. There were no persecutions in Britain during their century so they were spared the fame of martyrdom.

Near Cirencester, where once was the Roman city of Corinium, are the remains of many beautiful villas, and in one of these was found a cup inscribed with the Chi Rho of the Christians. Lavinia may have used it.

And in Corinium itself is a pavement of mosaic which depicts Orpheus playing upon his lyre. Birds and deer and little hares are gathered about him for no one could resist the music of Orpheus. But in the border of the picture at each corner is a chalice which was not there when Buvinda refused to throw water on the face of the god. And it is plain that this Orpheus was taken as a symbol of the Savior, the music of whose love drew all men to Him. And the chalices at the corners represent the cup which Joseph of Arimathaea brought so long ago to Glastonbury.

www.ingramcontent.com/pod-product-compliance
Lightning Source LLC
Chambersburg PA
CBHW050417260626
47156CB00003B/1048

* 9 7 8 1 9 5 5 4 0 2 2 2 4 *